SURVIVING
ASTEROID STORM
SUPER ELEMENT 126

By: Brian H. Cole, P.E.
2022/2023

Dedicated

Dedicated to my wife Patti Cole, who has helped greatly with book content, encouragement, and understanding. She kept me grounded as well.

Cover

The cover photograph is by Patricia Cole

Copyright 2022/2023

Notes to Super Element 126
Registration Number: TXu 2-347-384
Effective Date of Registration: September 29, 2022
Registration Decision Date: December 13, 2022
Plus
Surviving Asteroid Storm Super Element 126
Registration Number: TXu 2-362-333
Effective Date of Registration: February 26, 2023
Registration Decision Date: March 30, 2023

Original ISBN-13: 979-8-218129255

Edition 2 ISBN-13: 979-8-987660935

Printed In the United States of America (Amazon)

Book Preview

After the Big Bang occurred, and after standard elements precipitated out due to the high pressure and temperature of star-building and explosions of supernovas, an unusual element was created under rare conditions. This Element is so rare that it's only found on a few planets within our entire universe, and one of those planets is planet Earth.

......fast forward billions of years into the future.....

Asteroids, billions of years old, come crashing down on the Black Hills of South Dakota and into the eastern prairie. A free Band of Lakota Indians witnesses the most spectacular light show on earth. The light show lasted for hours while the Indian people took cover for their lives.

......fast forward 100+ years......

Soil erosion over the past 100+ years has uncovered many dark-rock outcrops on ranch land as well as on the Pine Ridge Indian Reservation. The locals accepted these dark-rocks as ordinary landscapes, but one young Lakota Indian man became more curious, and the results he found were literally from out of this world.

News of the Super Element brought fortune hunters from all over the country, and they descended on the Black Hills just like the gold rush days of the late 1870s. A modern Wild West begins, but it also has the modern dangers of adversary countries and inquisitive billionaires looking for a profit in the next significant invention.

Who owns this Super Element, and who will protect it from being stolen? In a "David vs. Goliath" situation, this small community of ranchers and American Indians from the Reservation stand up to enormous opponents. With help from others in and around the Black Hills, they fight for what is theirs and for the national defense of their country.

The book titled "Surviving Asteroid Storm Super Element 126" began billions of years ago when the elements of the universe were created. This new Super Element traveled in a cluster of asteroids for billions of years until some crashed onto planet earth. The story revolves around a strange dark-rock found in a poor rural area in South Dakota. The people of this community are strong, resourceful, and independent. They have survived harsh environmental conditions for all of their lives. Still, even they seek help when an astonishing material, found only in one area of our planet, attracts influential individuals and desperate countries. Help comes from a variety of odd sources, including bikers from the Sturgis Rally and an army of old pickup trucks.

Table of Contents

Introductions

This book starts with known physics and science and then slow steps into science fiction. This was done to make the book's science fiction part more believable.

Please meet the following people in this novel.

Or

Alternatively go straight to Chapter 1 and return here later for more information on the characters if needed.

- Ed lived his entire life on a 180-acre ranch that borders the Pine Ridge Indian Reservation. He inherited his property from his folks and learned how to live on this rugged land with little money. He is retired from working various jobs during his life and receives Social Security checks, which is just enough to survive. He knows all his neighbors, including many on the Reservation, and they know Ed as someone they can count on for help. Ed is not married and lives by himself, but when he was younger, he had a beautiful long-term relationship with his girlfriend, Opa.

- Shappa grew up in a small community on the Pine Ridge Indian Reservation. She was poor during her upbringing and was raised by her mother. She barely knew her father, but he did come around from time to time. Fortunately, others in her small community helped out, and she felt she had many adults she could depend on for help. Her small community was big on education, and she received a good education (K through 12) in Pine Ridge. Shappa loved geology, and that interest helped push her to want to go to college. She applied and was accepted at the South Dakota School of Mines in Rapid City, South Dakota. She ended up going into Civil Engineering with the dream of helping the Pine Ridge Indian Reservation move into more modern times.

- Chaska is about one year older than Shappa, and they grew up together in the same small community, but Chaska was raised only by his mother. He never found out what happened to his father, but he was lucky to have other adults step up in his small community. As mentioned in Shappa's introduction, education was crucial to their community. Chaska also loved geology, just like Shappa, and he also applied and was accepted by the South Dakota School of Mines. Chaska studied Geology, Mineralogy, and also Chemistry. He excelled at all of these subjects and stayed in school for his Master's Degree. During this degree, he realized the importance of something he found on the Reservation. He completed his Master's Thesis on this subject, setting off a Pandora's Box with danger and riches.

- The Lead FBI agent assigned to South Dakota is Chris. He was initially from Rapid City and was comfortable in this area of the country. Chris moved to Denver to get a job in the Denver Police Department as an Investigator. He recently changed jobs to the FBI in Denver, and this was one of his first jobs in South Dakota as an FBI agent. Chris had a rough start but had the right skills to succeed. The Pandora's Box created by what Chaska found on the Pine Ridge Indian Reservation set off a chain reaction of events, and Chris was thrown into the middle of it. His job was to keep the peace and protect a new national interest.

- Ryan grew up in Rapid City, South Dakota, and now lives with his wife, Ann, in Hill City, South Dakota. Ryan never had an education beyond high school and barely made it that far. He worked various jobs to survive and bought a small home in Hill City. Ryan loved to fish and hike in the Black Hills, and he developed a natural skill for mineralogy and structural geology in his search for gold. Ryan didn't get rich with gold, but he considered himself rich by meeting and marrying his soul mate, Ann. Together they earned more money, and he eventually bought a Harley-Davidson motorcycle. Ryan and Ann loved their new life and became regulars in Sturgis, Deadwood, and other places in the Black Hills. Ryan and Ann became well known as the kind of people to help those who needed help.

- Ann and Ryan are married. Before their marriage, Ann grew up in Rapid Valley, which is a community next to Rapid City, South Dakota. Ann is a beautiful lady with the same hopes and dreams as Ryan. She worked various jobs in Rapid City and Hill City and had a natural gift for sales and marketing. Her marketing ideas helped her career immensely, making her well-respected in Hill City.

- Maka is the sister to Chaiton. She lost her parents to a terrible car accident when she was young. She lived with her relatives in North Rapid and also had a great mentor with a lady named Jennifer (Jen), introduced below. Maka grew up hard but turned her life around and eventually became a Rapid City police officer. Maka and her brother Chaiton (presented below) were instrumental in helping the Reservation people and nearby ranchers and landowners.

- Chaiton is the brother to Maka. As mentioned above, he lost his parents while he was very young, but with the help of Jen and his relatives, he became a good, responsible man. However, he lived a party lifestyle in high school and hung out with a rough crowd. Although he had some difficulty in high school, he eventually took the lead from his sister and became a Police Officer in Rapid

City, but he also maintained friendships with his old high school friends.

- Opa was Ed's girlfriend when he was a young man. She was a full-blood Lakota Indian. They met at a very young age under challenging conditions and built a solid relationship over the years. She was the love of Ed's life and shaped him into the man he became. He misses her so much.

- Jen is married to Chris (new FBI agent) and is also from Rapid City. She became a nurse in Rapid and helped two young American Indian kids when they desperately needed someone (Maka and Chaiton). Jen loved these kids and helped them in grade school and beyond, but she and Chris moved to Denver for their jobs. Ann kept in touch with them and was there for them when they needed anything.

- Wichapi & Hotah were free Lakota Indians when the Pine Ridge Indian Reservation was created. They, along with their Band of Lakota Indians, witnessed the Super Element asteroids when they crashed into South Dakota in the 1800s. They both became a legend in this area of the country, and the stories of their experiences live on to this day. These stories influence modern-day astronomy.

- Rusty is briefly mentioned in this novel. He is a rancher living next to Ed and the Rez. Rusty remembers some darker history on the Rez from the 1970s when the FBI had a shootout on the Pine Ridge Reservation.

- Dr. Rock is Chaska's advisor at the South Dakota School of Mines. He is very confident in his abilities and helps the Rez, and nearby ranchers develop a fair price for the asteroid material

Chapter 1: ELEMENT CREATION

Billions of years ago, in deep space, and shortly after the Big Bang, the mass of the universe began to evolve. The building blocks of mass for celestial bodies are the chemical elements we learned about in chemistry class. As the mass from the Big Bang cooled, elements began to precipitate out, and the first were light (few protons), like hydrogen and helium. As these lighter elements clung together, the mass grew larger until the first stars were created, and gravitational pressure from these stars produced new elements up to iron (26 protons). These early stars would exist for billions of years. Eventually, they would collapse under their own weight, creating so much intense heat and pressure that they would explode into a "supernova". This explosion created super-hot spots that fused matter together, making the heavier elements on most planets today. However, that wasn't the end of the element creation within the universe. At a few locations within the universe, even bigger explosions created much more heat and pressure. These events were extremely rare and occurred when an exploding supernova star was directly in the path of an intense gamma-ray blast produced by a giant black hole. Events like this created an extremely rare but stable element much more significant in mass than anything shown on our current periodic table. The Element had an atomic number of 126 (126 protons), and it did not decay in seconds, days, or even billions of years as it would travel through the galaxy as an asteroid cluster (a group of asteroids of various sizes from the size of cars to small mountains). This Element would eventually be called the Super Element, and the properties and characteristics of this Element are nothing short of unimaginable.

The universe would continue to expand for billions of years as other newer stars and planets were created with the mass of old exploded stars. Debris (asteroids) from these exploded stars and asteroids made up with the Super Element would travel through the universe. Eventually, most asteroids, including the Super Element, would crash onto other planets or burn up near stars. One of the places that the rare Super Element would crash onto was planet earth. More specifically, the Super Element crashed onto our planet in what is now South Dakota in the United States.

Special References:

Cosmic Queries, StarTalk' Guide to WHO We Are, How We Got Here, and Where We're Going, by **NEIL DEGRASSE TYSON**, with James Trefil, Edited by Lindsey N. Walker, National Geographic Partners, 1145 17th Street NW, Washington, DC, 20036-4866 USA, Copyright 2021 Curved Light

Productions, LLC., Interior Design: Farris &Akkach.
Pages 133 - 135. Typically, superheavy elements
decay in fractions of a second, but nuclear theorists
predict that when element 126 is realized, it may
bring new discoveries in chemistry (Island of
Stability).

ALSO:
Wikipedia 11.12.2022
Unbihexium, also known as **element 126** or eka-
plutonium, is the hypothetical chemical Element
with **atomic number 126** and placeholder symbol
Ubh. *Unbihexium* and *Ubh* are the temporary IUPAC
name and number, respectively, until the Element is
discovered and confirmed and a permanent name is
decided upon. In the periodic table, unbihexium is
expected to be a g-block superactinide and the eighth
Element in the 8th period. Unbihexium has attracted
attention among nuclear physicists, especially in early
predictions targeting properties of superheavy
elements, for **126 may be a magic number** of
protons near the center of an **island of stability**,
leading to longer half-lives, especially for 310Ubh or
354Ubh, which may also have magic numbers of
neutrons

 ALSO:
Homephysics News
Superheavy Elements: Nuclear Physicist's Voyage
Towards a Mythical Island
TOPICS: Atomic Physics University
By LUND UNIVERSITY FEBRUARY 15, 2022
**Theories were introduced as far back as the 1960s
about the possible existence of superheavy**

elements. Their most long-lived nuclei could give rise to a so-called "island of stability" far beyond the element uranium.

Chapter 2: PREHISTORIC ASTEROID

A cluster of asteroids, created from old exploded stars, traveled for billions of years before being caught in the gravitational pull of our sun. This gravitational pull put the cluster of asteroids into an elliptical path that would take it around the sun, flung them out past Pluto, and then back to the sun again. This long elliptical path would take many years to complete, and this path was mostly the same for each trip, with only minor differences. Still, those little differences lead some asteroids within the cluster into collision courses with planets in our solar system. One such collision was on to earth about 65 million years ago. It was one of the large asteroids and smashed into what is now the Yucatán of Mexico. You may have learned that this impact caused the end of the age of dinosaurs. The Yucatán asteroid originated from a broken star that went supernova, and it was one of many within this asteroid cluster that were composed of common elements. However, this cluster also contained many asteroids with the Super Element. The remaining asteroid cluster stayed farther out of earth's gravitational pull, at least they did at that time, and remained in an elliptical path in our solar system for millions of years. Eventually, though, most of the asteroids would be caught by the strength of gravity of several planets, including planet earth.

Chapter 3: 1880 SOUTH DAKOTA

The Indian Wars of the late 1800s were nearly over, and the federal government was setting up reservations for the remaining Indian tribes. One reservation was Pine Ridge in southwestern South Dakota. Pine Ridge was a barren piece of property, away from the gold in the Black Hills. Back then, the land was not considered valuable, and it became an Indian Reservation. During this time, a small Band of free Lakota Indians were living in the southern Black Hills, just as they had done for hundreds of years. However, in recent years they had to travel farther from their homes to hunt for Buffalo. They were led by a man named Hotah and his wife Wichapi, and they had been forced to hunt farther from home due to the number of new settlers staking out home properties and gold prospecting within what was their old hunting grounds. On one particular hunting trip, the Band traveled way out east, past what is now the town of Buffalo Gap, and out closer to the newly created Pine Ridge Indian Reservation. On the evening that they arrived, shortly after sunset, this Band of Indian people prepared for their typical night's rest when one young tribal member shouted to look up at the sky. The entire Band looked up, and they were witness to a startling and somewhat frightening evening. What they witnessed were many asteroids entering earth's atmosphere and crashing deep into the Black Hills, and also near where they camped. It was like a modern-day war with asteroids rather than missiles flying through the sky with long tails of smoke and fire. Some even had strange noises as the fires crackled in the atmosphere. This event was a direct hit on earth from much of the remaining asteroid cluster that once included the Yucatán asteroid. The ground would shake when a large piece landed nearby. It appeared that most asteroids were crashing into the forested areas of the Black Hills as well as out where they were on the prairie.

The Band of Lakota Indians huddled close together and tried to find rocks or hillsides to hide behind, but that would not have mattered much when an asteroid hit. The noise was frightening when these large chunks of old stars crashed onto the earth's surface, and the explosions were enormous. Dirt was thrown for long distances, forcing the Band to cover their mouths to breathe better, and their eyes watered with the dust in the air.

This extreme light show lasted for hours and ended near midnight. By the end of this episode, the entire Band was on edge, and they could see several large forest fires deep in the Black Hills and on the prairie near where they were camping. As the night continued, several scouts kept watch for any fires that may be headed their way, but fortunately, rain fell, and the prairie fires were short-lived, allowing the Band to relax a little.

When daylight arrived, the Band witnessed animal behavior they had never witnessed before, with antelope running fast in all directions. The large herd of Buffalo they were following the day before was split into several groups and ran in different directions. Fortunately, the first hours of daylight helped settle things down, and by noon, the animal life and this Band of Lakota Indians started to settle down.

They could see large plumes of smoke coming from the Black Hills from their location in the prairie, but none seemed to be from their home location in the southern Hills. Most fires were from what is now the town of Hill City all of the way to Spearfish, South Dakota. This was some relief, but wind directions can change, and their home camp in the Southern Black Hills could still be at risk.

Hotah and other leaders decided to cancel this hunting trip other than any larger wild animals they could safely take while returning to their home camp in the Black Hills. But they were in for more surprises. On their way home, they passed several large craters that steamed with hot rainwater. At the bottom of each crater were glowing objects with sharp edges. Little did they know that these glowing objects were the Super Element from deep space, billions of light years away. The objects seemed unaffected by the heat generated while traveling through the earth's atmosphere. They were not melted and were only partly broken apart due to collision with the earth's surface.

This Band of Indians camped just outside of the pines at what is now called Buffalo Gap, South Dakota. It was a favorite location for them because it had a small lake for water and fishing and just fun cooling off from the hot summer days. They could still see smoke coming from areas within the Hills, but the smoke plumes were smaller and fewer. Rain was usual at this time of year; fortunately, they were getting some. Within a week, the smoke stopped altogether, and the Band thought it safe to head up into the Hills to their Black Hills camp. The camp was unaffected and safe.

Everyone was on edge for months and even years after this event, as they did not understand what had happened. Several within the Band tried to explain it by saying things like the lights in the sky came down to save them from the new prospectors and homesteaders, but nobody believed this. This was one of those times in history that had little explanation at the time, and it made them nervous for the rest of their lives.

During the years to come, nothing like this ever happened again, but from time to time at night, they could see lights streaking through the sky, and they would disappear just as fast as they appeared. This Band of Indians was the first humans to realize firsthand what these streaks in the sky really were.

During future Buffalo hunts, they would travel into the eastern prairie land again and past some craters created by the asteroids. It was always mystifying to walk past them, but over the years, some of these craters would be filled with dirt from erosion, and many were buried. Others would remain partially exposed, mainly if they were in drainage ravines. The stories of these asteroids were told amongst this Indian Band from generation to generation.

East of the Black Hills of South Dakota
Pictures by author, 11.23.2022

Bad Lands of South Dakota, Picture by Patricia Cole

Chapter 4: CURRENT DAY SOUTH DAKOTA

A man named Edward Zimberman struggled to
survive on his 180 acres of land located east of
Buffalo Gap, South Dakota. His property was
immediately adjacent to the western border of the
Pine Ridge Indian Reservation. Most people would
describe the land as barren or wasteland because it
was mainly grassland and open drainageways with
little to no vegetation. Even the Bureau of Land
Management (BLM) identified this ranch land as
needing many acres to support just one cow with
grass. Realistically this wasn't possible due to the lack
of surface drinking water and the unforgiving winds
that would often be deadly in the cold of winter. For
this reason, Ed had a few goats and several scrawny
chickens, and he had some outbuildings to protect
them from the elements. Fortunately, he also owned a
stock dam and associated lake that was initially
funded by the BLM, and this kept his animals with
water and helped feed his water well that he used for
drinking, etc. This small lake also kept him in catfish
that had a muddy but decent taste. Some trees also
started to grow here, and one cottonwood tree grew
fast. It offered shade in just the first few years, and it
became a favorite place for Ed to take a nap on a hot
summer day. When the tree grew tall enough, it
became the landmark for finding Ed's place and one
of the best fishing holes in the region.

. . . .

The climate in this area of South Dakota was
sometimes rigorous. A few winter months were cold

and challenging, but most of the year offered a comfortable climate, and Ed thought of himself as lucky to live where he did. He liked the Spring and Fall best, but the truth is he also liked the challenge of winter and the long hot summer nights out fishing for catfish and bullfrogs in the moonlight. Ed had never traveled out of this area, so he didn't know of any other climate. It was what it was, and he accepted and even enjoyed the weather changes. Having lived here all his life, he was ready for anything that came his way; it was normal for him.

The landscape in southwestern South Dakota is of three main types. The Black Hills is, of course, forested, including several spotty areas of Black Hill Spruce trees outside of the main Black Hills (Hills for short). Eastward from the Hills, the land changed to grasslands with rolling hills. Farther east, this grassland landscape slowly changes to that of the Bad Lands of South Dakota, which is large swaths of clay soils of various colors. Large drainage channels within this area that cut through the colorful clay layers create unusual, rugged beauty with little vegetation. When wet, this clay soil is the type that clings to shoes and becomes as slippery as ice. The water in Ed's stock dam comes from one of the larger channels, and this more significant channel has several unusual rocks poking through the soil layers. The rocks are dark in color and add a mystique to the landscape. The locals called these rocks "dark-rock" to distinguish them from other landscape features.

The dark-rock was not always exposed to sunlight and had been covered with local soils since the first few years after they arrived over 100+ years ago. When Ed was a young boy, he didn't remember seeing many dark-rock at all, but over many years of rain, snow, and wind, these mystery rocks have become partially exposed. The one thing Ed did notice is that the dark-rock doesn't erode. Once he noticed the rocks, he was surprised that they didn't crack or change at all, and one time Ed remembered a dark-rock being hit by lightning, and during that moment, the rock disappeared, but he just thought it was his imagination. The locals have accepted these unusual rocks as ordinary landscapes because it has taken decades for the rocks to have been partially uncovered. The dark-rocks only come to mind when visitors comment on them.

......

Ed knew all of his neighbors, including other ranchers and the American Indians that lived on the reservation (Rez for short) within a 50-mile radius of his property. Knowing his neighbors was enjoyable for him, but it was also good to know them all for help in case of emergency. Almost everyone got along, even though they were hardened and independent individuals that knew how to survive on the land, with a solid 4-season climate.

The land that Ed lived on was passed down to him from his parents, and his parents inherited it from his father's side of the family, so this land has been in his family since it was homesteaded near the time the Rez was established. For this reason, he knows those on the Rez and surrounding ranches and farmsteads as well as a country person can. Ed genuinely likes his neighbors, from going to school with many and hunting and fishing with others. Ed enjoyed the solitude of living alone and particularly liked the dark night sky, but occasionally he felt a deeper loneliness. Ed also wanted to keep in contact with his neighbors, so he would often drive to either the town of Pine Ridge or Buffalo Gap to drink a few beers. He always knew someone when he went there, and this is where he learned of the news in his area and just kept in touch with his community. After all, living miles from your nearest neighbor gets a little too lonely. Because of his drive back, he only stayed a few hours, though. Also, trouble sometimes occurred later at night after people had too much to drink, and he avoided trouble. However, this wasn't always the case. When Ed was younger, he was full of himself and often got into fights, and in this low-populated part of this country, that meant he had fist fights with just about everyone his age, which made his friendships stronger. He knew he could count on his neighbors, and they knew that they could count on him.

Ed had been alone for most of his adult years, and he accepted that, but when he was younger, he had a long-term relationship with one of the neighboring Indian girls named Opa. Their relationship started under emergency circumstances when they were about ten years old. A fast-spreading grass fire on Ed's folks' land put them on the move to outrun the flames. The heavy winds and the smoke made it hard to breathe, but Ed's father and mother managed to hook up the horses to the wagon and get them out of the way of the flames (they couldn't afford a car then). Things happened so fast, and the smoke was so thick that his folks didn't know exactly where they were when they broke out of the smoke and flames and into safety. It turned out that they had crossed onto the Rez, several miles from their homestead. They went to the nearest home and were met by a girl named Opa and her parents. Opa and her parents had been watching the smoke from the grass fire and were preparing to leave until the wind changed, moving the fire away from their home. Opa and her folks welcomed Ed and his parents, and they all sat down together for some water and delicious homemade bread. Although they didn't live that far apart, they didn't know each other, and it was good to meet them finally. Opa spoke excellent English, but her folks were more used to talking in Lakota. In either case, the conversation was good regardless of these communication obstacles. It also gave Opa a chance to talk more, and she enjoyed having visitors, which they rarely had. Opa and her folks didn't see white people on the Rez, so this was kind of strange, but Opa's folks knew of the white ranchers near the Rez and were told that they were good people. The adults talked some more while Opa showed Ed their property. It included some interesting landscapes, and one of those dark-rocks was also there. Opa and Ed climbed on the rock as if it were a playground, and they hid in a hole on one side of it. It was smooth too, and they used it as a slide. But the fun was over after they could hear Ed's father calling for him. The fire had burned out in this area and smoldered on burnt grasses. This indicated that it was reasonably safe to go back to check out the damages. Ed and his folks thanked Opa and her family for the hospitality and went home. Over the coming years, Ed would never forget Opa, and he would visit her occasionally.

Fire trucks just didn't exist in this area, and few people owned cars because of cost, so fires of this size were free to continue until they burned out naturally. The fire caused a lot of damage, and Ed's father and mother needed to complete the necessary repairs to make it livable again. Until that was completed, they lived outside in tents and in one of the outbuildings that were previously used for the animals.

......

Ed's father tried to raise cattle on his 180 acres, but the ranch land just wasn't reliable for grazing. Some years produced enough grass for grazing, and other years were more challenging, but the most difficult part of raising cattle here was the cold winter wind, and that's why Ed's father built a couple of outbuildings. These buildings kept the livestock from freezing, but after two years of cold winters, Ed's father gave up his dream of being a self-sufficient cattle rancher. He took what little money he made from selling the cattle and bought pigs, goats, and chickens, and with the outbuildings already in place, it worked out much better. The pigs bring in money when mature, the goats produce milk, and the chickens hatch sufficient eggs for selling. Ed received a rancher's education from his father and mother and the struggles they had in trying to make a living. It wasn't easy, but it also taught Ed that he didn't need a lot to be happy in life. Ed grew up similar to the Indian kids on the Rez. He respected the weather and enjoyed the climate but knew not to underestimate Mother Nature. He also learned to respect all life and that even though ranch animals were a food source, they also needed to be treated with fairness, not cruelty, and to give thanks for the nourishment they provided. Much of the Indian ways were integrated into the lives of the surrounding ranches. It just made sense when living close to nature.

When Ed turned 12 years old, he thought about Opa more. Sometimes he would walk miles to get near her house to sit next to the dark-rock, watching to see if she would be outside. He would stay there for hours and eventually walk back home. Sometimes he would see her and her folks playing some game outside in front of their home. It was kicking a homemade ball of some sort to gain points between a couple of rocks. It looked fun, and all three of them would laugh and have fun for hours. Occasionally he noticed Opa look over at the rock where he was, and he thought she could see him, and she did. She knew he was there most of the time and loved to know he was there. Her folks took notice, too, and just let things evolve naturally as long as they knew their daughter was not in any harm.

On rare occasions, she would walk over to the rock when she saw him there, and they would talk for hours. Her folks supervised from a distance, of course, but they eventually learned that Ed was a good and respectful young man, so they occasionally had him over for meals.

Ed was an excellent young man because he was raised to respect others, and his folks taught him good ranching practices. When Ed was 13 years old, his folks gave him a black and white pig for an FFA project (Future Farmers of America). He raised that pig, and it became his own pet for years. Ed did everything from feeding it and making sure it had water. The pig would follow Ed everywhere he went, even in the house, which was okay with his folks. The pig was housebroken (it didn't poop or pee in the house). Eventually, this pig grew enormous and couldn't even get through the front door, so it stayed outside with the other pigs. All of the pigs flourished with reasonable care, and within a year, they had a large passel of little black and white pigs running around the ranch. It was fun to watch them all.

At the end of his FFA pig project, Ed was to sell his prized pig for as much as he could get, and that year his pig would bring a lot. The pig was sold to a prominent pig farmer, and he told Ed that he would use the enormous pig for mating with other female prize pigs to have superior offspring. This made it easier for Ed to sell his pig because he loved his pet pig, but it was big now, acting differently and much more independent.

With the money he won from his prize pig, he bought a used motorcycle, a Honda 50. It was his motorcycle that helped him see Opa more. He even rode it in the winter, freezing his hands for miles, but she was worth the trip, and they built a wonderful relationship.

He had never felt the way he did about anyone before her, and she felt the same about him.

Ed and Opa didn't go to the same school even though they lived only a few miles apart because the Rez had their own school in the town of Pine Ridge, and Ed went to a one-room schoolhouse that was closer to Chadron, Nebraska. After school, Ed would ride over to Opa's, and they studied together. Sometimes he would pick her up, and they went to Ed's place so that Ed's folks could also get to know Opa. Both families were happy with this relationship.

At 14 years old, Ed and Opa were a couple, and by 15, they were usually together. Both Ed's parents and Opa's folks knew they couldn't stop this cute couple from experimenting, so they had the appropriate discussions and warnings. They knew that both of these young adults would be careful because they were raised with understanding and respect. Both Ed and Opa would not want to disappoint their folks.

At age 16, Ed and Opa ruled their own worlds. Everything was easy for them, and they were as happy as ever. They were doing well in school and enjoying life together and with their parents. The two families became closer, and this helped them live in this harsh environment by sharing tools and labor as needed. Both families bought vehicles, so they had dependable help with transportation. Opa's family purchased a used Ford pickup truck (2-wheel drive), and Ed's folks bought a used Ford Bronco (4-wheel drive, 4x4). Both vehicles had specific uses. The truck could obviously haul things, and the Bronco's 4-

wheel drive could get to locations where a 2-wheel drive couldn't. For this reason, both families helped when needed.

At age 17, it was well known that Ed and Opa would get married soon, and they were already married by some standards. They were openly planning their future together after graduating high school. Both families offered areas for building a homestead site, but they chose a plot of land on Ed's folk's land. His folks offered 10 acres bordering the Rez. Given that Opa was full-blood Lakota, they could legally enter Rez land from their 10 acres. With this land, they would need a mobile home or manufactured home, a water well, and a septic. Power lines could easily come off the poles going to Ed's folk's house, so this was cheaper, but everything else was not, so they worked various jobs to earn enough to take out a home loan. Ed and Opa planned on getting a loan for a home by the time they were 18 or 19 years old.

When they were 18 years old, they wanted to be officially married, both on the Rez for her folks and off the Rez for his folks, two weddings. The modern days of the 1960s were just different from the old ways, and both Ed and Opa embraced some of the changes. Life was good.

Unfortunately, a tragedy occurred when Ed's folks took Ed and Opa to Rapid City for a day in the city. They didn't like the city that much, but it was an exciting change, and they felt sorry for all those people that had to live there, but everyone has different lives, and the people of Rapid City seemed happy and pleasant. On the way to and from Rapid City, they needed to take Highway 79, which was two lanes back then, one in each direction. They all had a great time in the city and were on their way home, just north of the intersection to Buffalo Gap, when a drunk driver crossed the intersection and ran head-on into their old Ford Bronco. Ed was the only survivor.

Ed woke up in a hospital in Hot Springs, South Dakota. He had been in a coma for three days and then stayed in ICU (intensive care unit) for five more days, including two days with hospitalized delirium. When Ed finally came back, Opa's folks were there with others from the Rez and a few other nearby ranchers that lived close to Ed's home. The outpouring of support was tremendous, and Ed was grateful. He was eventually sent home when he could manage living by himself, and the drugs helped with that a lot, but the drugs finally wore off, and Ed wasn't going to be dependent on man-made medicines. Natural medicine was his way, just as it was for Opa, but nothing helped as the drugs did, and Ed struggled through it.

It was horrible to go back home. His folks were dead, and Opa, the love of his life, was gone in a flash. Ed went into a deep depression and was holed up on his ranch for about a year. Other ranchers and Opa's folks tried to contact Ed, but he went into seclusion as well, not seeing anyone except to pay bills or get food. The year was hell on earth for Ed.

Ed doesn't remember much about the first few months after the accident. He slept most of the time and ate infrequently, but he remembers getting a letter from the government about the draft, so he registered for the Vietnam war. Ed had hoped to get a low number to fight and die in combat because life just wasn't worth living anymore. Ed received a number that was too high to be drafted, and he didn't want to volunteer, so that ended that.

The seasons came and went, and Ed stayed on his property. He thought nature had to heal him eventually, so he spent much of the year outside, even in winter. Ed loved a live campfire and only went inside during sub-zero temperatures. The cold somehow made things better, or maybe he felt he deserved the discomfort of coldness. Nights were getting easier for him as he curled up in many blankets and stared up at the beautiful dark sky each night. The stars made him feel better, and he began believing that death wasn't the end. The universe is so incredible; anything is possible. He just didn't want to live this physical life without his loved ones.

Ed decided it was time to die one cold winter day, so he took a walk without wearing winter clothing. He walked all the way to where he could see Opa's house and broke down there. It was there that something wonderful happened. A snow squall came through the area, and it was blizzard-like. He could not see very far in front of him as he started to walk back to his place, and as he walked through the snow, he felt the cold entering his body, and numbness replaced the feeling in his hands and feet. Then he came across the rock outcrop that he and Opa played on years ago. It had a small opening on the downwind side, and he crawled in. It was warmer inside, and he curled up in the fetal position and fell asleep. His dreams were strange but realistic in bright colors. He was reunited with his folks and with Opa, and they talked about the accident. They told him that he needed to continue in the physical world and know they were now in paradise. They said they would wait for him and that it was not time for him to die. He had exciting experiences to be a part of, and then the dream started to fade away. His parents were gone, and he was alone with Opa. She told him she loves him very much and they would be together soon. When Ed woke up, the snowstorm was over, the sun was shining brightly, and the air was warm. Ed looked out of the small opening and saw a wedge of geese fly over him in a beautiful formation, only about 15 feet from the ground. He crawled out of the opening and could see Opa's house, so he walked toward it. Ed was a mess, with dirty clothes, long wild hair, and a long beard, but even in this condition, Opa's folks could tell it was him. They both came running out of the house and hugged him until they all fell to the ground. Ed was back again and with family. Ed considered them his parents, and they considered him their son, as they all healed their emotional scars.

After this horrible nightmare was over, Ed was welcome everywhere on the Rez. He was one with the Lakota people forever on the Pine Ridge Indian Reservation.

East of the Black Hills of South Dakota

Buffalo Gap, S. Dak., Pictures by author, 11.23.2022

Chapter 5: NEIGHBORS

In the 1990's Ed often found young Indian kids fishing on his lake. Ed had plenty of catfish in the small lake, and he knew the kids would have fun catching them and providing food for their families. He didn't mind this at all, and he or one of his neighbors would often cross property lines in pursuit of game animals. It was just a part of being a good neighbor.

Over the years, Ed got to know all the kids and watched them grow into strong young adults. He fished with them often and knew their folks as well. They became good neighbor friends, and on several occasions, they shared deer jerky and vegetables from their gardens in appreciation for the catfish. Ed was good friends with everyone in the neighborhood where the Indian kids grew up. It was a close nit community, and Ed was included. The kids saw each adult in the community as an extended parent. Ed was the only white man to be accepted like this.

Two of the kids had always been interested in the rocks and geography of this area of South Dakota, and they both kept collections of minerals that they found on their land, as well as other places where their folks took them. The older male was Chaska, and his female neighbor was Shappa. They grew up together with several others, and all lived in a small housing development, like a small neighborhood in a town, except there were no stores, churches, or taverns, just older homes with a common water well and septic system and many broken down vehicles.

.....

Shappa and Chaska were born one year apart, Shappa
being the youngest. Single mothers raised both, but
Shappa's blood father would show up occasionally,
and he would bring presents and some money for
Shappa's mother, so she knew who her birth father
was, but he didn't spend much time with them.
Shappa's mother told her that her father wanted to be
free, but later, when she was older, she understood
that to mean he wanted to be free to drink whenever
he wanted.

As Chaska grew up, he would ask others about his
father, but all he'd get was an old joke, like, "He went
to get some cigarettes in his Ford, but it probably
broke down somewhere." At first, he believed it and
worried about his father, but after a while, he just
gave up asking. The joke changed, too, because there
were just as many Fords as Chevys, so sometimes
they would say he drove off in his Chevy, and that's
when Chaska figured out the joke.

Shappa and Chaska had other friends in their housing
development and had a happy childhood under the
circumstances.

Most of the kids in their neighborhood also grew up
with just one parent, but since they were such close
neighbors, they helped each other as needed, and this
unity provided a good upbringing for the kids, except
for schooling. Learning was problematic because
most of the adults never had formal training. The

adults were experts at survival and living naturally on the land, but they never went to a traditional school, at least not for any length of time. They bartered for an old van that they used to drive the kids to the town of Pine Ridge for their education five days a week. Each parent took turns driving the kids to school, and they all did this with enthusiasm. They knew that education would be the way out of poverty. Education on surviving on the land was essential to them, but they also realized that the world was changing and changing fast. They all wanted the best futures for their children, even if they stayed on the Rez or decided to move away from the Rez.

They didn't have television, but they had a radio that could pick up Rapid City channels in the day and KOMA from Oklahoma City at night. They liked the current rock and roll channel's the best, but also listened to talk radio. They still had plenty of extra time on their hands, so reading became a good past-time as well, and this helped them with their education.

As young teenagers, Shappa, Chaska, and some of their friends would venture out from the village in search of rocks and arrowheads, and they found a lot of good ones. They came across some weird stuff too. One day they came across a snake on a ledge. As they looked closer, they could see that the head of the snake was just a skull, but the body of the snake still had the skin, and the skin was still moving, just like the snake was alive. Chaska took a stick and moved it some, and that's when a bunch of maggots fell out. It was pretty gross and shocking, too, but these adventures got Shappa and Chaska out into the surrounding hills and eventually interested in rocks and geology.

Other adventures around their housing development turned up some interesting fossils, so a couple of their friends became interested in Paleontology. On other adventures, they found arrowheads, but one time was most interesting.

In the Spring of one year, when the snow melts and erodes away dirt and clay, new fossils and exciting things are occasionally uncovered. Shappa and Chaska were about 14/15 at the time and were older than most in their group. What they found was the butt of an old rifle sticking out of the muddy hillside. They dug further and uncovered the whole rifle, then saw the bones. It belonged to an old union soldier. The bones were somewhat gone, but the uniform, leather belt, and boots survived. The gun was severely rusted, as was the knife. They told the older folks about the find, and they gave a proper burial, even though it was possible that this man may have killed their relatives, but no one would ever know for sure. During that incident, the young people learned of past finds on the Rez. They were sworn to secrecy and then driven to the town of Oglala on the Rez. Near town, they walked to an old cellar made of old logs. They walked down the stairway and opened the door to a musty, earthy-smelling room. The wooden room had no electricity, so they used flashlights and a gas lantern. In the middle of the room was a large wooden table, and on the table were many items wrapped in oily rags and plastic bags. The elders grabbed one long package, and they all went outside in the daylight to see what was inside. The package had several items and sounded like metal as it was unwrapped. To the amazement of the young adults, two old muskets and one pistol were uncovered. The elders explained that they had found many such items since their people were forced on the Rez. They didn't want the white man to know about these, so they took good care of them in secrecy. They never used any but kept them in case they needed to defend themselves on the Rez, but the white man left them alone on the Pine Ridge Reservation for all of these years. By the early 1900s, the Indian people could buy their own guns, so newer weapons were purchased for protection, but these older ones were stored away, just in case. The table in the cellar must have had 20 different wrapped packages, so there were a lot of exciting finds from the past. The gun and knife they had just found were also placed in the cellar on the table, but they were rusted beyond repair.

As Shappa and Chaska aged through high school, they became romantically involved. At this time, they decided to go to the same college. They both were accepted at the South Dakota School of Mines, which is only about an hour and a half north. Chaska chose geological engineering as a major, and Shappa chose civil engineering as her major. Both graduated with good grades. Chaska went for his Master's degree, and Shappa decided to work with the Bureau of Indian Affairs (BIA) to improve the way of life on the Rez, such as roadways, clean water, sewer systems, communications, etc. Shappa envisioned a modern-day town with a hospital and an Indian-based manufacturing company that paid good wages. She had big dreams, and that was her motivator. On the other hand, Chaska was fascinated with the chemistry of minerals down to the quantum level. His fascination and dedication made him one of the most promising students in his class.

Both Chaska and Shappa had secured some student grants, but most of the money they used for college came from student loans. They took those loans seriously and were very frugal with the money. They both rented rooms in an older home near the college. The house had four bedrooms and one bathroom that they all shared, and they shared the kitchen too. They shared a phone bill, but the homeowner paid all other bills. It wasn't fancy, but it was clean and safe.

Both Shappa and Chaska worked part-time jobs for extra spending money and to stretch the loan money as far as possible. They were frugal with the loan money, so it would be easier to pay off once they were in the workforce.

Chapter 6: AN UNEXPECTED VISIT

Four years had passed since Chaska, and Shappa started college at the School of Mines. Ed was in his 60s, but he was still strong as a bull and felt good. While in town, others would comment on how young and fit he was at his age. That's when Ed's humbleness and shyness emerged, and he would joke that it must be something in the water. All kidding aside, Ed and several others wondered why the catfish in Ed's stock dam lake were so much bigger and healthier than all the other fishing holes in the area. Ed would even barter with his catfish catch, so he fished a lot in the summer, and that's where he was when he had unexpected visitors.

It was the early evening after a beautiful South Dakota day, and Ed parked his old pickup truck next to his favorite fishing spot on his small lake. He backed the truck up to the water's edge so that he could fish while sitting on the tailgate, just as he'd done a thousand times. "No rain tonight," Ed thought because he was looking forward to fishing until midnight again. Light cool breezes followed the day's heat, and he felt great. He was fishing for just half an hour when he heard a vehicle drive up. It was Chaska and Shappa, holding fishing poles and carrying a six-pack of Grain Belt beer each and large bags of Doritos. Ed hadn't seen his young neighbor friends for years and was thrilled to see them again. Ed said, "What took you so long to visit me!" That led to hours of conversation and catching up.

They all drank beer and had a good time fishing and talking. Friendships like theirs picked up where things were left off, except Ed could see more maturity than before, and that's when Chaska asked Ed if he could take a sample of the dark-rock on his property. The Rez also had many locations of dark-rock, but Chaska knew of a thinner outcrop in which he could get a small sample. Ed immediately said, "go for it, my friend, but that rock is hard as steel ."Chaska agreed and said he would drop by later that weekend. Chaska then said that he and Shappa needed to go for now to see their families and others in their small village. Chaska had not been home for a long time because of his dedication to his studies, and Shappa was very busy with job interviews and final exams. She also told Ed that she was returning to the Rez with a new job, but she told Ed not to say anything about this because she hadn't told anyone in her home village yet.

Chaska and Shappa told Ed to keep the remaining beer in trade for the catfish they caught, and then they took off for the village. Ed, a little drunk by now, was happy to see his friends again and continued to fish for a few more hours. It was such a pleasant evening. Ed ended up sleeping in the bed of his truck that night, looking up at a thousand stars in the sky and knowing that no place on the planet could be more perfect.

Chaska and Shappa went back to their small neighborhood village. The entire population came out to greet them. Both had just graduated with Bachelor of Science degrees, and Shappa surprised them when she explained that she was returning to the Rez. She had just accepted a job at the Bureau of Indian Affairs (BIA) and would work as a Civil Engineer on roads and utilities. She was moving to the town of Pine Ridge to be closer to the office and road maintenance department. Chaska then explained that he was staying on at the South Dakota School of Mines to get his Master's degree and that he would investigate the dark-rock on the Rez.

Many people attended this joyous occasion, including many from other towns on the Rez, but most were from the larger town of Pine Ridge. Two of their own people don't graduate from the South Dakota School of Mines every day. They knew that this school was challenging but gave an education that paid more than Harvard for some years. Graduates are offered excellent livable wages right out of school.

Celebrations such as this brought out the best of the Rez. People would bring their favorite foods, most from their land. Foods included seasoned rabbit, deer, antelope steaks, and many types of vegetables from home gardens. One family got a few Buffalo from the annual Buffalo Roundup from last September. They briefly thought about butchering one for this celebration but quickly changed their mind. It was a bad idea because they would instead try to rebuild the herd on the Rez. Buffalo are too rare these days and must be allowed to reproduce. They brought deer jerky instead. Shappa and Chaska brought catfish from Ed's lake. There was so much food that it was hard not to stuff yourself.

After eating, the celebration included speakers from senior members of the Rez, as well as elders. Each had encouraging words in both English and Lakota. They wanted people on the Rez to speak both languages to not forget the past and look toward the inevitable future of working in a predominantly white population. When it came to the older speakers, stories of success were told of the past. This, of course, included the adventures of Hotah and Wichapi. These were some of the favorite stories, but the small neighborhood that Shappa and Chaska lived in did not always see these elders, so many of the stories were new to them. One story was about survival from the fire rocks in the sky. This story was new to Chaska and caught his interest. After the speakers finished, Chaska introduced himself and conversed with all three elders from Pine Ridge. Chaska was shocked at this story, and the conversation continued for hours into the evening. Chaska wondered; was the dark-rock he was going to use for his Master's thesis the same material as the fireballs?

Back at the celebration, everyone in their community was glad to hear that Shappa and Chaska were staying in South Dakota. They had heard that most South Dakota School of Mines graduates leave South Dakota for out-of-state jobs. This good news spread throughout the Rez and surrounding ranches.

Chaska dropped by Ed's place a day later to get the sample rock. He told Ed that he was going to use a mass spectrometer and other equipment to determine the rock's chemical makeup, but Ed didn't know what a mass spectrometer was, and he didn't ask either. They said their goodbyes, and Chaska headed toward Rapid City and the School of Mines.

Chapter 7: THE SCHOOL OF MINES

As expected, the following week was extremely busy with classes, labs, studying, homework, and scheduling time for the mass spectrometer. Chaska required a subject for his Master's thesis, and the dark-rock would be perfect. He knew something was strange with the rock and looked forward to starting his experiments but first things first.

Chaska's sample was big enough to separate into four pieces, and damn it, that rock was hard. One part was used for what is called a thin section, which is made so thin that it's only a few molecules thick and made transparent to see any crystallization or other mineral structure. Another sample was used for testing with heat to determine the melting point. Another sample would be used to establish strength (compression and tension). The fourth piece was dedicated to the mass spectrometer and would also be used to test various electromagnetic beams and electricity levels. The material was found not to be radioactive, so testing did not require any special equipment for handling. However, it did emit warmth.

The mass spectrometer was scheduled for the following week, so Chaska decided to do other types of testing on the samples first.

The first test that Chaska performed was to determine the melting point. He was surprised at a melting point of about 10,000 degrees Fahrenheit, but even more shocking was that the material didn't expand or contract during heating. Given these results, he then took this same sample and exposed it to extreme cold. To his amazement, the sample did not expand or contract again, which was extraordinary.

Chaska then tested the material for compression and tension and found that this material had the best properties for both compression and tension, better than both hard rock and metals. Given the surprising result of temperature, compression, and tension, this material would be perfect for different construction types. This material would be of enormous benefit to the space industry as well.

The following week, Chaska had access to the mass spectrometer. His advisor assisted him because he had used this machine sparingly. The results were astounding because they didn't match any chart data for any known element or isotope, so they sent the sample into the mass spectrometer repeatedly, with the same results each time. The machine was working perfectly, so why such strange results? This material was completely undiscovered.

Chaska's advisor was also his professor on several undergraduate and advanced degree subjects. His peers respected him throughout the academic world. His name was Dr. Rochester, but Chaska and the other students called him Dr. Rock. Dr. Rock had been at the School of Mines for over 20 years and had a reputation for being absolute and confident. During field trips, he used an ink pen for notes and sketches when everyone else used a pencil (to correct errors). Dr. Rock didn't make errors; he was that good.

To see Dr. Rock excited about the results from the mass spectrometer was a spectacle. Not even long-term staff assistants ever saw him so surprised and happy, but this was Chaska's project, and Dr. Rock ensured he was only assisting. However, this was bigger than any master's thesis, so he controlled how the project would proceed. First, he wanted the samples secured at all times. Then he called a meeting of all senior staff and graduate students in geology and mineralogy. The meeting was scheduled after classes ended for the day, at 5:00 pm.

The meeting occurred in a large classroom in the geology building on campus. Word got out that Dr. Rock was excited about some project, and this news was so surprising that the meeting attracted nearly everyone invited. Dr. Rock started the meeting by introducing Chaska and then gave Chaska the floor to talk about the incredible results of the newly found rock.

Chaska explained his Master's thesis on a rock he found on his home's property, and then he described his recent experiments. Chaska said, "I thought I might have found a new combination of crystallized minerals that bonded in a super tight fashion, but I now think this is a completely new element not on our current periodic table. The properties differ substantially, offering great potential for super strong building materials." Chaska continued, "I will be conducting further experiments and testing in the coming months," and that's when Dr. Rock interrupted. Dr. Rock said, "The reason I brought you all together is that this has huge potential, and it's like nothing I've ever seen or heard about before. I'd like you all to help Chaska if you'd like, but it's his project, and he will be the Lead. No one but him will have credit for finding and recognizing the potential for this material, but if you help, you will be given credit as appropriate." Everyone in the room knew what he was talking about and wanted to be a part of this venture.

As the meeting ended, Dr. Rock commented, "I want you all to understand that this might be one of the most significant discoveries in the last 100 years. As a result, it is important to keep this information out of the public eye. We have no idea what could happen if this news gets out". Then the meeting ended, and Chaska was surrounded by people that wanted to help. It was one hell of a day.

Dr. Rock suspected the information about this new Element was getting out too quickly, not just to other colleges and universities in the United States but also worldwide. Unfortunately, news travels fast when something like this is discovered. As a precaution, Dr. Rock warned Chaska of a potential media blitz and that Chaska should not tell anyone where he found the samples. Dr. Rock also suggested that he arrange an alternate residence location if the media gets too aggressive.

The samples of this newly discovered Element were hidden under lock and key, and the School of Mines hired additional security. This plan worked for the next few weeks, as much more was learned about this material. It was confirmed to be a new element with

126 protons and was found to be stable and compact. The mineral structure was highly complicated, but it did explain why the Element didn't expand or contract during temperature changes. They also found it to be a great conductor of electricity, but not temperature. Heat or cold did not transfer through the Element very well, but experiments with electricity caught everyone by surprise.

One sample was connected to a 12-volt battery, with positive on one side and negative on the other. When power was turned on, most of the sample became partially transparent. Chaska increased the power, and the Element became more transparent. When the power was turned off, the material returned to its original opaque condition.

Another astonishing characteristic of this Super Element was that most electromagnetic frequencies are absorbed by the sample when beamed at it. But there was one main range of electromagnetics that was an exception: the visible range for human and animal sight. Visible light is electromagnetic, but this visible range of electromagnetics was not absorbed but reflected instead so that animals could see it. This meant that no form of radar (or radio wave) could detect it, but it could be visibly seen.

Dr. Rock immediately contacted the Dean of Electrical Engineering and all senior staff of the School of Mines. Within an hour, Chaska demonstrated this shocking characteristic to the top tier of the School of Mines. Many were then seen on cell phones with their counterparts at the Colorado

School of Mines, Stanford, Yale, Harvard, Cambridge, and others. Shock and disbelief were the typical reactions.

Chaska was quickly becoming well-known, but this celebrity status was to have terrible repercussions.

Chapter 8: WARNINGS FOR HOME

It took a couple of days in the spotlight before Chaska realized the dangers for his friends and family back home. It came to him as a dream just before he woke up. The dream was disaster and death to his loved ones because other countries were trying to steal the Super Element from the Rez and surrounding ranches. He woke up in sweaty sheets.

Chaska isn t one to have knee-jerk reactions, but it took him only 10 minutes to load up his truck for a trip back to the Rez. He quickly got on highway 79 toward Hot Springs and drove as fast as he could without speeding. He knew that the sheriff would have a car somewhere on highway 79. The last thing he needed was to get pulled over by the sheriff. He traveled cautiously down the highway while calling Shappa and Ed to arrange a meeting of all neighboring ranches and the Rez. Chaska said he was going straight to Ed's place and would describe the dangers they could experience. He said he would be there in about an hour.

Shappa and Ed were stunned by what Chaska was saying but took his advice, contacted all neighbors, and told them of the emergency meeting. Fortunately, the weather was good because Ed's house couldn't hold them all.

The next hour was a chaotic mess of vehicles pulling up to Ed's place and people bringing out chairs, boxes, and whatever so everyone had a seat. It was July, so the sun stayed up longer in the evening, and

Chaska arrived at the time the last remaining neighbors came as well. It was a group of about 20 total neighbors, 11 from the Rez and the others from surrounding ranches. Everyone knew one another, and it was a good time for many to catch up on the news in the area.

Once everyone settled in, Chaska said some danger might be coming to their lands. Chaska explained the happenings of the past few weeks and the incredible discovery of the new Element and its exceptional characteristics. He told them he had just realized the impending danger and wanted to warn them that many people, companies, and possibly adversary countries might want this Super Element. The group was surprised, to say the least, and listened with intent. After Chaska's explanation, one of the ranchers, Rusty, brought up another potential problem. Rusty said, "What about our government? Remember the two FBI agents killed on the Rez in the 70s? What if our government tries to take over our lands to get this new Element?" Rusty referenced a shoot-out on the Rez in 1975, where two FBI agents were killed during the American Indian Movement (AIM). They were shot with an AR-15, and over 100 bullet holes were found in their vehicle. Arrests were made, and it turned out that the killer had a previous and unrelated arrest warrant from Wisconsin, but rumors ran wild back then, and suspicion of the FBI exists today. Also, the federal government doesn't have a good reputation in these parts because all pay taxes, but little to no benefit comes from these taxes, so Rusty's comment hit a chord.

Chaska then said, "Rusty is right! We need to think of all that might want the dark-rock and be suspicious of everyone that we don't know who travels out here. In the meantime, I'll contact a couple of police officers that I trust in Rapid. They might have some suggestions." Ed then spoke up and suggested that they all exchange current telephone numbers so that the entire group could be contacted and warned if anything happened.

The meeting ended after an hour, and they agreed to meet at Ed's place every Friday to discuss updates and have a few beers. They all hoped that this was an overreaction, but just in case, they were starting to arrange a regional defensive militia, similar to the Minutemen during the revolutionary war. They called themselves the Dark Rock Defense Community (DRDC).

Chaska then drove back to Rapid around midnight. His mind was running wild with crazy thoughts on his way back home. Everyone at the meeting was having a hard time accepting this possible danger.

Chapter 9: FRIENDS

The next day Chaska went to class as usual, but he could not get the thoughts of yesterday's meeting out of his mind. He eventually just gave up on school for the day and drove to the Rapid City Police Department to talk with a friend he had since starting at the School of Mines.

Shortly after Chaska started college, he became friends with an American Indian lady named Maka Red Elk. She was near his age and had grown up in North Rapid. Maka and her brother Chaiton both became Police Officers a few years earlier. Chaska became good friends with Maka, but nothing romantic.

Chaska arrived at the Rapid City Police Station and asked for his friend. Dispatch contacted Maka, who was out on patrol at the time. Dispatch relayed a message from Maka to Chaska to meet her at the Firehouse Restaurant for an early dinner, so they met up after work.

It had been a few of years since they were last together, and since then, they both had increased responsibility. Maka got a new job with the police department, and Chaska finished up his undergraduate degree. They caught up on things first, and then Maka asked Chaska why he wanted to meet. Chaska told her the long version of events and asked if she had any suggestions.

To Chaska's surprise, Maka already knew about the situation because the Rapid City police department was in the early stages of coordinating with the FBI on some experiments at the School of Mines. Chaska's face changed immediately with this news, and Maka was shocked at his reaction. Chaska was starting to panic, and that's when things got dire. Chaska said he feared for his community back home.

Maka thought about it briefly and then told Chaska she had an idea. She reluctantly confided in Chaska that her brother had old connections with tough biker friends from high school. Maka told Chaska that her brother keeps these friendships low-key because he's a policeman, and these friends are not precisely law-abiding. However, these same bikers had helped many others in difficult situations before, and she suspected that they might be of help. She said that she would definitely talk to her brother about the situation. This offer helped Chaska relax a little, and the remainder of dinner was fun for them both, talking about old times and their recent achievements.

The next day, Maka called Chaska with some good news. Her brother did contact his biker friends, and they were excited to help, mainly when they heard that the FBI was involved. She said these bikers were going to Sturgis now but would help after the Sturgis bike rally ended.

That same day Chaska informed his family and friends about the FBI contacting the Rapid City Police Department. He also told them that he knew some other friends in Rapid City and Sturgis who might want to help them protect the dark-rocks. Chaska then settled down and returned to class and his investigation of the Super Element. It was early August, and Chaska had completed all his experiments and was now writing his thesis. He would finish the requirements for his master's degree very soon and could turn all of his attention toward his home community, both on the Rez and off-Rez with the ranches.

Chapter 10: DRDC UNITED

By the first week in August, the DRDC (Dark Rock Defense Community) was getting stronger, more organized, and more fully united. They were all friends before, but now they were practically family. Everyone went out of their way to help neighbors plan and protect the dark-rock outcrops. They developed an early warning system that included a systematic telephone protocol. Shappa (on the Rez) and Ed (on his ranch) would be contacted first, and then other nearby ranches and reservation communities, expanding to ranches farther away from the dark-rock outcrops. The outer ranches were on the lookout because they would see any unknown visitors first.

Each family had both pistols and long guns. These pistols and rifles were mainly passed down from older generations. They were in sound to excellent condition because good gun safety and care for these weapons were learned at early ages. The AR-15 rifle was rarely seen in this community due to cost. Almost everyone worries about outsiders, such as the government trying to get their land. Still, nobody thought it necessary to buy military-style weapons, and everyday life didn't require this type of weapon either. A gun clip with 13 cartridges is enough for hunting or target practice.

On the Rez, they started to bury dark-rock outcrops, and this was a good idea for the rocks that were not out of the ground very far, but rocks protruding more than 4 feet were much more difficult and could have hidden better. They mapped all the known locations of all dark-rock on the Rez and assisted nearby ranchers with the same efforts. They also included detailed pictures of each rock. In this way, if a rock was stolen, they could prove ownership.

The landscape at each dark-rock location was analyzed for lookout locations, and the best and stealthiest sites were identified on the maps, which each DRDC member had.

Few had battery backup power because this was expensive, and most members didn't have much money, but they ensured everyone had enough firewood to last through winter if required.

Food and water, plus any prescribed medicines, were supplied and stockpiled as needed for any DRDC member, and they accumulated much more just in case more help arrived.

With the supplies, weapons, maps, binoculars, flashlights, phone communication, wood for the fireplaces, and gassed-up vehicles, the DRDC was as ready as they could be, even though they didn't know what threat could occur. Even if nothing happened, this preparation would help with the coming winter.

Chapter 11: FBI

The FBI met with the Rapid City Police Department for office space and possible backup assistance. They also coordinated with Ellsworth Air Force Base for a possible airlift of supplies and workforce. These were only precautions, though, because their assignment was to keep the peace and protect the residences and natural resources. However, this information was not available to the DRDC. Most of the people involved thought of the FBI as bad news. Maka wasn't informed about this information, so she still had apprehensions about why the FBI was involved.

The FBI had a small army of individuals because a federal physicist determined that this new Element would attract bad actors such as Russia and the radical side of Iran. In addition, the sneakier countries like China would no doubt want their hands on this Super Element. The FBI knew these countries would stop at nothing to get this Element. They knew it would radically change the balance of military power and space exploration. Whatever government controlled this Element would dominate forever. For this reason, other countries would spare no effort to get their hands on some of it. It's that important.

The FBI had 50 agents and 25 SUVs driven directly from Denver, Colorado, and Washington, DC. Of course, they were black, but they didn't mind the locals knowing they were there because they were there for protection. Also, any negotiations for purchasing this Super Element would be direct and above board. They knew the Super Element was for national security, and they would not allow the open selling of the material, but this was America. The FBI was instructed to offer a fair price for all known dark-rocks.

During the last few days of the Sturgis motorcycle rally, the FBI notified Chaska that they wanted to meet with him at the School of Mines, but Chaska refused and said that any meeting would occur at a ranch near the Rez. Chaska was referring to Ed's home; he had previously OK'ed this with Ed. The FBI was a little taken aback by this because this was just a friendly first meeting. They soon realized they were now considered a potential threat, so they softened their tone. The FBI can come across as intimidating.

The FBI agreed to meet at Ed's place at noon on the last day of the Sturgis Rally.

Chaska then informed Shappa and Ed of what was happening, and those two then told the rest of the DRDC. Chaska also told Maka and Dr. Rock and asked Maka and Dr. Rock to attend if they could. Maka couldn't go due to work, but Dr. Rock would be available.

The news to Maka set off a domino effect. When she called her brother Chaiton, he called his biker friends. His biker friends were having their final party at the Buffalo Chip tavern in Sturgis, so they felt no pain. One of his friends got up on the bar and loudly announced that the FBI was trying to take property away from their friends 100 miles from here and put out the word for help. The Buffalo Chip exploded in excitement, with many wanting to help and others spreading the news to taverns and bars all over Sturgis. They arranged to meet at the Buffalo Chip the next day, the last day of the Sturgis Rally, the same day the FBI was meeting Chaska and the others at Ed's place.

The next day arrived, and everything and everyone was now in motion. All 50 FBI agents packed their SUVs and ordered 50 subway sandwiches from a nearby Subway restaurant. It was 10:00 am when they left the hotel.

Chaska was also in motion, picking up Dr. Rock in his truck. They were on highway 79 by 9:00 am, giving themselves a couple of hour head start to set up the meeting site outside Ed's place. All was going as well as it could be. The entire DRDC group was present, and most were packing weapons. They wanted even ground on this particular meeting, and nobody would tell them what to do, EVER. This was their land and their dark-rocks.

The FBI showed up on time and in force. It was an unusual sight to see with so many black SUVs and just as many old trucks and Jeeps from the locals.

The FBI gathered on one side of a long broken-down table, and the DRDC on the other, including all American Indians and local ranchers for a 50-mile radius.

The lead FBI agent was named Chris, from the Denver office. Chris was specifically selected for this job because he was from Rapid City and previously worked for the Rapid City Police Department. He and his partner Jennifer both grew up in Rapid and started their careers there, but they both found pay increases with new jobs in Denver, Chris with the Denver Police Department, and Jennifer as a head nurse. Chris recently changed jobs to the FBI in Denver, and this was his first chance to show his bosses that they made a good choice in hiring him.

Chris started things off by introducing himself and his other lead personnel. He then apologized for bringing such a considerable force but thought it necessary to cover such a large area. That's when Chaska asked, "Why are you expecting to cover our land area? This is our property, and you must be invited to be here." Chris agreed immediately, as he didn't want this to escalate into a divisive meeting. Chris was talking about protecting the property from outside sources, and this was new news to all locals, but escalation was occurring due to the suspicion of the DRDC by some of the FBI that thought of these people as hicks. Chris didn't know this, and the tension was as thick as mud. From the corner of his eyes, Chris saw that several agents were moving laterally to flank the DRDC slowly, and he yelled, "STOP!" That's when hell nearly broke out on both sides, and everyone pulled out weapons. The DRDC was outgunned, given the military assault rifles and automatic weapons that the FBI had. Fortunately, both sides hesitated, weapons pointed. The only sounds were of the wind lightly blowing dry grasses, a few birds, and a loud frog croak from the small lake behind Ed's stock dam.

Rapid City, S. Dak., Pictures by author, 11.23.2022

Chapter 12: THE STURGIS EFFECT

After nearly a minute of silence, Chris started to speak calmly. He told his leads to back the FBI agents up, and that was when they heard the thunder of hundreds of Harley-Davidson motorcycles. The sound came from miles of nearby asphalt roads near Ed's place. In the lead were Chaska's friends from high school, about half American Indian and half white. They wore dark sunglasses, no helmets, with their long hair flying back in the wind. Behind them were hundreds of bikers. It was a sight to behold.

The FBI backed up, and the DRDC took a well-deserved breath. The tension on the DRDC side was somewhat relieved because the FBI no longer had the upper hand.

The bikers took position around the DRDC and then flanked the FBI on both sides, giving the FBI agents a taste of their own medicine. Chris told his agents to stand down, and this was the right thing to do because it gave him a chance to tell everyone the true intentions of the FBI, which is that they are there to protect them and their property. They were not there to cause problems or to seize anything, but he also told the DRDC that they would not allow this Super Element to be uncontrolled or sold to other countries. Chris said, "let's take a break now and put down our weapons. Let's get to know one another better without weapons". He then instructed his agents to disarm and put their weapons into the SUVs. Chris ordered half his agents to stay at the SUVs and others to be available for conversation with the DRDC.

Chaska wasn't the leader of anyone in the DRDC, but he also disarmed himself and asked others to do the same, and most of them put their weapons away.

Chaska and Chris then started to talk directly with one another, with everyone else listening in. Within the first half hour, the DRDC members became more comfortable with the FBI's intention, but some FBI agents still had concerns. After a couple of more hours of conversation and explanation, Chris said they were going back to Rapid for now. He said that he could see that the large group of bikers was enough to scare off any adversary, and the FBI then went back to Rapid with the promise to be back the following day under better circumstances. Chaska agreed and thanked Chris for controlling the situation.

After the FBI left, the DRDC and bikers all cheered loudly. Things ended beautifully, thanks to the biker's perfect entrance. Conversations were many, with loud excitement. Then Chaska jumped up on the table and got everyone's attention. He said that he believes Chris and the FBI, but they still need to negotiate the cost of the dark-rocks. He said that the real value was unknown but that any agreement would need to be 100% agreed upon by all DRDC members. He mentioned that Dr. Rock was here to help with that. Chaska thanked everyone and asked Ed if the bikers could stay on his property that night. Ed, a man with few words in a group setting, said, "of course, they are very welcome."

A party at the stock dam lake lasted until way into the night. Everyone that stayed on Ed's property was well prepared for camping since most were camping up at Sturgis, and it was a great night, too, with clear skies and reasonable temperatures.

Sturgis, South Dakota, Picture by author, 11.23.2022

Chapter 13: BIRTH OF THE AMERICAN TEAM

The following day was much better. Chris called Chaska at 8:00 am and said he was giving his agents a few hours off due to the stress from yesterday but that they would be at Ed's by 2:00 pm. Then Chris asked what the DRDC meant, and Chaska explained it meant Dark Rock Defense Community. Chris responded, "Chaska, that's a great name for your supporters, and Chaska, I meant what I said yesterday about protecting you and your neighbors." Chaska simply said, "Thanks, see you this afternoon." However, there was more than one reason that Chris couldn't be there that early.

Chris gathered the Team leads and all of the other FBI agents. What he saw yesterday, with the beginnings of flanking the DRDC, could have been disastrous. Chris said, "If you don't think of these people as equals, you must return to DC and I mean today. Nobody on my Team will think of themselves as better than these country people. They have ten times the survival skills and can withstand harsher climates than any of us. So, if you disagree, please pack your bags and go home. I will not advise discipline if you leave, no questions asked." Ten agents left for DC that afternoon, and 40 agents continued to Ed's place in half of the vehicles, leaving the other half at the hotel.

When they arrived, all the FBI agents exited the SUVs wearing new button Henley T-shirts with one front pocket. The shirts had DRDC on the front and

Dark Rock Defense Community on the back. They were navy blue, and the agents' carried boxes of these shirts. Hundreds of them were made for the entire community and the bikers. Chris was trying to show solidarity with the DRDC and the bikers, and the shirts were well received. It was important for this American Team to be united because other countries were planning undercover operations simultaneously.

The tension between the FBI and the DRDC was gone for the most part. The FBI stayed on Ed's property for the rest of the day to answer any questions. Chris said he'd like some agents on site and asked Chaska to let him know. Chris told Chaska there was no rush and said he felt good about the biker protection that the DRDC had then, but he also said the offer was open for when they were ready for the FBI help. It was a good day, and as evening approached, the FBI left for Rapid City.

After the first week, most bikers returned to their home states. The Sturgis Rally was over, and they felt a sense of pride in what they were a part of, particularly with the now-united American Team. About 25 bikers stayed and contacted friends and families in Rapid City, Sturgis, the Black Hills, and surrounding areas for food, water, and other supplies to set up a better defense for the DRDC. It would be a long winter, and they wanted to get set up early. As a result, pickup trucks full of support supplies came from Rapid City, Chadron, Sturgis, Hill City, Newcastle, Deadwood, Lead, Belle Fourche, Hot Springs, all towns in and around the Hills, and even from as far away as Denver, Minneapolis, Casper,

Cheyenne, Scott's Bluff, Sioux Falls, Watertown, Yankton, Mitchell, Aberdeen, Pierre, as well as other Indian Reservations in South Dakota and neighboring states. It was like a town was being built with tent structures and port-o-pots.

The collective American Team called DRDC was born. Now it was time to plan for every possible attack from adversary countries. They knew it would be bold to try to steal the dark-rocks in place, particularly in the middle of the United States. As a result, the Team thought it could happen during the transport of the material, but the Team also had another problem. They needed to find out where all of this dark-rock was buried. It was obviously on Ed's property and many places on the Rez, but where else?

On the Rez, rumors of an 1880s Lakota Indian Band told of many asteroids crashing in the middle of the Black Hills to the Pine Ridge Indian Reservation. If true, then securing the Super Element just became nearly impossible.

Chapter 14: NEGOTIATIONS

The morning after the DRDC and the FBI agreed to work as a team to protect the dark-rock, Chaska had a short telephone conversation with Chris and told Chris that before a single ounce of material was removed from the Rez or Ranches, they needed a formal contract on price and remediation on the property after removal. Chris was happy to oblige and set a date for the next day at noon at Ed's place.

Before meeting with Chris and the FBI, the DRDC met to agree on a few things first. The ranches outside the Rez would have one voting member per property, and the Rez reserved the right to negotiate separately. However, they might accept the price negotiated by the other ranchers. Then they started to discuss the price. Dr. Rock explained that the price needs to be based on the estimated quantity plus the projected use. Both of these were unknown and very difficult to estimate. As a result, Dr. Rock suggested a scaled cost, with an initial amount based on rough estimates of material and uses, and then the price would scale up when better info was learned. This way, money could be realized now, and not all dark-rock will be sold cheaply.

The federal government agreed to the terms; after all, as long as they made some sense, how could they refuse and still be considered fair to the owners? But Chris insisted on storing all unsold dark-rocks in a federally protected area. Price negotiations for unsold rocks would occur when owners agreed to sell more dark-rock. The ranchers agreed to this, and unsold rocks from ranches would be fully documented by their lawyers and stored in an undisclosed location by the federal government. The Rez disagreed with their unsold dark-rocks and said that any unsold Rez rock must be stored in a vault located explicitly on the Rez. The federal government didn't like this at all but had little choice. However, the federal government agreed to build the vault on the Rez based on federal specifications, which was agreeable with the Rez. After all, the vault cost would not be cheap, so the Rez would save money, plus the hassle of constructing the vault. The vault was huge inside and had two-feet-thick concrete with steel reinforcement walls, plus a thick solid steel doorway the size of a large overhead garage door. The federal government would also supply the locks. The agreement also included remote sensing cameras and alarms, to which the Rez and the federal government had access.

The vault was built just west of the little town of Oglala, well within the Rez. Nobody in their right mind would try to steal the dark-rock from so far in the Rez. Pine Ridge was in the middle of the country, which made stealing these rocks and trying to get them out of the country even more insane. In fact, many tourists would not go on the Rez for fear of being arrested within a sovereign nation such as Pine Ridge. Many rumors were spread over the decades about vehicles breaking down on the Rez, and when the owners came back the next day with a tow truck, the vehicle was jacked up, with all wheels missing and anything of value gone from inside. True or not, this gave the impression that the Rez was lawless, so only people would go through the Rez if they knew the ways of the Rez like Ed did.

Chapter 15: CALM, CLUES, and CONTRACTS

The remainder of the summer was well-earned calm on the Rez and local area. However, the potential danger was on the mind of every person in the know of this new Super Element. The DRDC continued with the Friday meetings, and the membership increased considerably. The DRDC included:

- The local Rez and local ranchers.

- The FBI.

- About 28 bikers (3 bikers came back to help from Tyndall, South Dakota; Beulah, Wyoming; and Sundance, Wyoming).

Also, occasionally some Hills and Rapid City locals would attend to offer help and keep themselves updated.

The events from last August made the local news and briefly the national news until the federal government asked the media to help keep the Super Element out of the news for national defense reasons, and the responsible networks complied. A few anti-government news outlets claimed their rights to freedom of speech and continued to broadcast the situation. Still, little could be done about that since the news was already out there, and any adversary group and country already knew about the Super Element.

At the first Friday meetings after the incorporation of the FBI and bikers into the DRDC, most of the talk was about unknown locations of dark-rock. The rumors from the 1880s were more than interesting, and many asked for more info on this. Three American Indian Elders agreed to describe what they knew of the stories from the time of Hotah or Wichapi. All of them were direct descendants, meaning that their grandparents actually lived in the 1880s and remembered Hotah and Wichapi telling the stories when they were kids. The stories were absolutely true, and the three American Indian Elders went into great detail. You see, they all heard these stories over and over again, and they memorized them. Only minor differences occurred between the stories that the elders told. They even pointed in the direction of the fires caused by the asteroid collisions, in the general direction of Hill City from Ed's place.

The stories were fascinating to hear, and the entire DRDC was captivated while they were being told. The stories were described by all three of the elders, and when differences occurred, they were discussed in full, but none of these differences amounted to much of anything.

The whole story is as follows:

It was a warm fall day when the Band of Indians started out toward better hunting grounds east of the Black Hills. Hotah and Wichapi led the way and started the trip on horseback. They didn't have enough horses for the entire Band, so they traded off walking and riding. Travel was slow, but this was an exciting trip for them, and it was nice to see a different landscape. The Band totaled 56, including the younger children. It was to be a weeklong camping adventure, and if they found Buffalo, only the strongest warriors would go on the hunt. Fortunately, they had enough horses for each of the warriors because being on foot would be much more dangerous. If they did make some kills, the entire Band would be involved in dressing out the carcass. Then, every horse would be used to carry the meat back to the home camp in the Black Hills. Everyone would walk back except for the youngest, who could ride the horses with the meat. That was the plan, and they had made these trips many times in the past, at least once per year before winter.

They didn't always know where the Buffalo were, but they could often see signs of them during the first day's travel. This year they saw plumes of dirt and dust in the distance on the second day, so they headed off in that direction.

It was a beautiful fall trip and the most reliable season for non-violent weather. It was clear skies, and it wasn't too hot. The few trees they saw were changing colors from green to yellow and red, and there hadn't been a frost yet, so prairie flowers were plentiful. The birds were gathering in groups to fly south for the winter. The Band didn't hunt these smaller birds and saw them as entertainment. From the sights, sounds, and smells, nature was at its best at this time of year.

Along the way, they picked up edible plants and hunted mostly rabbits for hot cooked food in the evening. Otherwise, they brought water and prepared food for the trip but knew where to go for watering holes and fishing.

By the second night out, they had a good idea where the Buffalo were, and they camped just far enough away not to alarm them. They also stopped early in the day to rest up and plan for the hunt on the third day. The horses were given special care with extra water and food, and the Band was settling in for another comfortable South Dakota evening, and that's when things began to change.

The sun had nearly gone down, and shadows were long. One young boy noticed a cloud-like streak in the upper atmosphere just before darkness. It was strange to see such a thin cloud, and the Band talked about it some, but it wasn't that unusual to see different clouds, so they started to settle in around campfires. Then, when darkness set in, another young boy shouted, "Look up!". He said it in such panic that the entire Band looked skyward. Several fiery balls were coming down in the distant Hills, and others were coming down fast toward their location. It was a frightening sight.

A few men covered the eyes of the horses to keep them calm, and the rest of the Band huddled next to dirt and rock ridges, but they all kept watch of this extreme spectacle. It wasn't just the fire that they experienced. Several fireballs came in so close that they could hear the fire cracking, and each left a streak of smoke behind it; when they crashed nearby, the ground would shake. This noise upset the horses, and several men attended to them and kept them from running off.

The sky was filled with streaks of smoke, and the fireballs kept coming. This light show lasted for hours, but by midnight the last of the asteroids had arrived, leaving only the fires, and there were many. The prairie was on fire, but fortunately, the winds kept them away from the Band. The middle of the Black Hills was also in flames, and the southern area of the Hills was starting to cloud up and was not visible to the Band of Indians. The far northern Hills appeared to be okay. The fires were confined by a wide area from the middle Hills out into the prairie where the Band was camping.

Fortunately, rain occurred in the southern Hills, and the clouds slowly rolled into the prairie where the Band was camping. The rains shut down the prairie fires, but the fires in the middle of the Hills remained.

The elders then explained what the Band experienced on the trip back to their home in the southern Black Hills…..

With the Band safe from fire, they decided to end the hunting trip and return to their home camp in the southern Hills, but they took some time to enjoy the rains first. Rain was not expected on this trip, but it sure was welcome. It ended after half an hour, leaving bright blue morning skies and clean air. They took their time packing up and eventually turned for home. On the way home, steam rose from many areas and caused an eerie environment with occasional low-hanging fog. The Band finally made it home, but the center of the Hills remained on fire for about a week. What a godsend; they had survived, and the horses were safe.

The details of the story told by the three elders were captivating. It made those listening feel the tension of that day, and everyone could understand why this story was kept alive since then.

No one doubted the authenticity or truth of the stories, and some clues were very welcome. For instance:

- The fires were in the general direction of Hill City, as seen from Ed's place

- If they could verify fires from the 1880s near the Hill City area, this would offer a smaller search location. This task was very doable too, and the FBI took on this task. The FBI would also research any records kept by towns or communities in the Hills at that time.

- Hotah and Wichapi said the fires didn't affect the southern Hills.

- The fires didn't burn long, meaning they were localized.

This information wasn't very much, but way more than they had before. The Elders were thanked by everyone and given official T-shirts showing they were now a part of the DRDC.

The description was detailed enough to make a person see the situation in the mind's eye and was better than written communication because of the excellent presentation of the elders. Now the FBI knew of the enormous task of locating and protecting the asteroid rocks in the Black Hills, and Chris knew he needed local help for this and a lot of it. Chris knew that more agents would not be the answer because they would not be trusted like locals would be. For this reason, he let the question sit for a few days to get his thoughts together. He can't afford to make a mistake with this problem because he knows he wouldn't get a second chance.

During the next Friday meeting, it was learned that one of the DRDC bikers, nicknamed Toe-blade, lived in the Hill City area. Toe-blade got this nickname from a kegger he attended near Sheridan Lake back in the early 1970s. One of the things they did back then was to stand face to face and then throw knives out from where they were standing, and if the blade stuck in the ground, the other person would need to keep one foot in place and then put the other foot out where the knife was sticking. One time, Toe-blade threw the knife into his big Toe, causing the entire party to crack up laughing. That's when his nickname stuck.

Chris started to ask some questions to Toe-blade (Toe for short) about the Hill City area. It turned out that Toe was very respected in Hill City because he had extensive knowledge of the entire region. Toe was a friendly guy and knew almost everyone in the area where he lived. He didn't mind his nickname and enjoyed the story behind it, but his real name was Ryan, so that's what everyone called him, at least most of the time when not in the bar. Speaking of the bar, Ryan told Chris that he knew just about everyone there and in Hill City and would know if someone was from out of town, and this gave Chris an idea.

The next day Chris called his DC office. It was Saturday, but someone was there 24/7/365+, which meant 24 hours per day, seven days per week, and 365 days plus per year (every day of the year). Chris wanted to know if he could bring on 28 contract employees and needed background checks on them all before next Friday. The names and details were exchanged, and Chris asked one more thing. "Can the FBI help these people create their own self-employed company (LLC)"? The answer was "Yes" to that question, and the Small Business Administration (SBA) helped make this a quick reality.

At the next DRDC meeting, Chris offered contract positions to all 28 bikers. All they had to do was to create their own business with the SBA, and then the contract work was theirs, for $5,000 per month plus health insurance costs. The job requirements were very specialized and perfect for these bikers, plus they could keep their current jobs as long as they stayed in their assigned town for at least five days per week. Oh, and the job required a very special security clearance. It allowed for past misdemeanor and felony convictions as long as the individual was found forthright to the FBI. After all, the info obtained from this assignment wasn't going to a courtroom. No, the information collected here was for national defense. Here are the details....

- Each biker was assigned a base area of the Hills in which they were to observe unusual behavior.

- The biker in each area would have a few beers in local bars for observation purposes; yes, this was a job requirement.

- Weekly reports were required in writing but could be in the form of an email.

- If something strange is noticed, then Chris must be alerted 24/7/365+.

- Safety is most important. Follow all laws, and don't get caught. If drunk, take a taxi or Uber.

- Meeting other contract bikers was encouraged for unity and good cover.

- Restaurant eating was required but reimbursable.

The contract bikers (sometimes referred to as contractors) were either deployed to the town where they live within the Black Hills or, if they were not from the Hills, they were sent to other towns not already taken by another contractor. All the main communities were included in the Hills, and the larger populated places had multiple contractors, like Rapid City and Spearfish.

At the same time as the deployment of the contract bikers, the FBI hired geophysical companies to scan the entire Black Hills for anomalies and to research old fire burn areas from the late 1800s. This tasking was a considerable undertaking, and it would take months. The FBI also hired air surveillance of the Hills but weren't the only ones.

Concurrent with the events above, the federal government completed negotiations for the dark-rock Super Element. The agreement was for all amounts found on the Rez and Ed's property. The contract was subject to complete privacy and confidentiality. It can safely be said that Ed and the Pine Ridge Indian Reservation are now multi-millionaires, and news of this spread like a South Dakota wildfire.

As of this agreement, the Super Element had not been found on any other properties, but that was expected to change considerably. The government set up a Hot-Line for reporting the finding of more dark-rocks, and the FBI asked the state of South Dakota and Congress to pass laws requiring reporting when finding any dark-rock. These laws were requested to keep this material under the control of the United States, such that no other country owns any. This material was that important to the federal government.

Word of the Indian Elders describing the asteroids within the Black Hills was becoming of more interest than the dark-rocks on the Rez and Ed's place. It was well known that the FBI was protecting the dark-rock on the Rez and Ed's place, so few prospectors went there. It was the cover of the forest in the Black Hills that was more attractive to those that were prospecting illegally. For this reason, the attention shifted dramatically toward the Hills, making the Rez and surrounding ranches much safer.

With a contract in place, the federal government started planning to process the Super Element found on the Rez and Ed's property.

Chapter 16: MATERIAL PROCESSING

The dark-rocks on the Rez and Ed's property were all identified with ground penetrating radar (GPR) and geophysical vibration prospecting trucks to look for anomalies in the ground. This process worked well; within weeks, they had a 3D map of the underground. This map clearly showed the Super Element asteroid material's location and approximate size.

Now the government needed to figure out how best to prepare the material for transport to Detroit, Michigan. They chose Detroit because large unused manufacturing buildings were already in place and could be re-tooled to melt down the material and form it as needed. Detroit would be the location for all processing and manufacturing of the material in any shape or form required. The federal government was already purchasing old warehouse properties and other old vehicle plants, but getting the material to Detroit was the real challenge.

The 3D image showed the approximate size of all dark-rock, and most were transportable via semi-truck or train, but some were too large and had to be broken up. The breaking of the material was challenging but doable. The government contracted this work to one of the large stone-crushing companies, and it turned out that an excellent company was located nearby.

Transport to Detroit was a scheduling and planning nightmare. Each truck or train required armed escorts.

During each stage of transport to Detroit, the caravans of trucks and the military security entourage received advance notice of schedules and any issues. They had 3 to 4 carriers at most times, and all had aerial support and local police or sheriff escorts through populated areas. The first transport was fake to test the process. Then the actual material transports started, with one every other day. Each carrier continued, stopping only for refueling. Drivers were switched out, and support vehicles changed every 8 hours.

Within two months, much of the dark-rock from the Rez and ranchers' property had been relocated to Detroit, except for unsold Rez rock stored in the vault on the Rez. Various banks and credit unions completed payments to the Rez and ranchers.

The FBI then leaked information that all dark-rock was removed, and nothing remained except the rock in the vault on the Rez. Then the vast majority of the FBI switched attention to the Black Hills.

Black Hills of South Dakota with buffalo herd in foreground

Chapter 17: INTRUDERS ON THE REZ

News of the new vault on the Rez eventually made it to foreign countries. Most countries knew of Indian Reservations and heard they were poor and lacked security and police. This understanding gave the impression that stealing the dark-rock from the Rez would be the easiest way to acquire them. However, it would be impossible to get such large and heavy objects out of the Country without being seen, but that didn't stop eight men from Louisiana. Actually, none of these men were from Louisiana, but that's where they were when they gathered one day every week. These men were part of a small militia. They met once a week to drink beer, smoke cig's, and shoot guns, for "protection and defensive reasons only, of course." They had shady connections that allowed them to purchase fully automatic Uzi weapons. Each militia member had one, plus anything else they wanted, but most just supplemented the Uzi with a pistol of one kind or another. Most were Colt 45 or Smith & Wesson 9-millimeter. They camped at a spot in the boonies where few people went. Here, they would talk and plan for events of an oppressive federal government that wasted their hard-earned tax money. What they believed was pure exaggeration, but it was very real to them and kept them united.

Bill was the spokesman for the group, and he owned a small construction company in a neighboring state where five of the militia members worked for him. His business was successful because he and his employees stayed employed, but little profit was realized. However, Bill's construction company had a lot of equipment, including two large dump trucks, a side-dump semi-truck, one front-end loader, a large crane, backhoes, etc., along with other tools for roadwork and construction of small structures. Bill and his guys loved working on vehicles, and most of them owned 4x4 jeeps for various years. Bill let his guys work on their own vehicles in the shop on weekends, and since they all owned Jeeps, they knew how to work on them well. They were all good, experienced mechanics.

Two of the other militia members were brothers. One lived on his broken-down boat, and the other rented a small place nearby with a heavy-set woman that lived with him part-time. They were usually unemployed but did get some labor work from time to time that paid them in cash. They also made money selling guns they received through their contact in Mexico.

All of these men had failed marriages but had a lady that they visited once in a while. None of them married again. They would rather drink beer, work on vehicles, or go fishing. Fishing was another reason for the weekly meetings in Louisiana.

Bill was the only one of the eight that was of some success, and that's why the others followed Bill so much. Bill also had more money, so Bill funded most of the cost of the militia.

When Bill heard about the vault holding the valuable dark-rock on an Indian reservation, he became very interested and brought this to the attention of the other militia members. He said it would be a cakewalk to blow a hole in the vault and then use his crane to lift the rock into his side-dump semi-trailer. This idea was an immediate hit with all militia members, and the more beer they drank, the better the idea was. We are going to be rich, they said!

Bill pulled out a detailed map of the Indian Reservation, and they all studied the map. It didn't take long before they had the plan. They would travel up to Rushville, Nebraska, and stay the night. Around midnight, two jeeps would drive up past the town of Pine Ridge to where the vault was located. They would place explosives at the door and blow it off. Then they'd attach thick cables to the dark-rock and drag it out. At this time, the crane and side dump would be on-site. Then, after loading, they would take another road toward Chadron that took them out of the Rez and over the border between South Dakota and Nebraska. They would have two large dump trucks waiting for them at this location. Then they would crane the rocks into the two trucks, leaving the side dump empty. They would do this in case someone saw the side-dump trailer on the Rez. Then it would be homeward bound and millionaire status. "What could go wrong" Bill would say, "After all, this is just a poor old Indian Reservation, and why would any state care if something was stolen from the reservation anyway."

Bill and the guys were proud of their plan and couldn't wait until it was time to start. They were going to take their Uzis and pistols, too, in case there was a gunfight, and they knew that they would have the upper hand in any conflict because they had been planning for the defense of an abusive government for a long time.

Bill waited for a hot and dry forecast in Pine Ridge, South Dakota. Finally, after a couple of weeks, the day came, and they had a solid ten-day forecast in late October. Bill immediately called the militia together, and all eight men took off in two dump trucks, the crane truck, the side-dump semi-trailer, and two 4x4 jeeps, plus they had enough weapons and ammunition to kill an army.

It took three days to get up to Rushville, Nebraska, where they checked into the motel. This was going to be a quick job, so they didn't take much food or water, just enough to get through the next day, then they pre-parked the two dump trucks at the get-away location at the Nebraska-South Dakota border (BIA Highway 41) that evening.

At midnight Bill and the guys were off and traveling north toward South Dakota and the Pine Ridge Indian reservation. Every vehicle had a cell phone and walkie-talkie in case they didn't have cell phone coverage. The jeeps went first to confirm the vault's location before the bigger trucks arrived, and all went well. The vault was easy to find because of the media coverage of this unusual dark-rock. They cut the wires to alarms and video cameras and even painted over the lens of the cameras just in case, and by 3:00 am, they were set up to do the blasting. All the vehicles were aligned for a quick escape, and all the weapons were loaded and ready for a fight or confrontation if needed.

At 3:10 am, the blast was loud enough to wake up the entire town of Oglala, just east of the vault, and it did. After the blast, the militia team learned what the good design of this vault was. The metal door remained, and only part of the concrete vault was cracked open. The militia had done its best to get inside, but they could barely see inside the vault, let alone get large rocks out.

They failed; now what? Bill told everyone to get in their vehicles and that they would escape via their original plans. The escape plans were to go back a different way than they came in, via the town of Pine Ridge. Instead, they would travel west on paved highway 18 for a short bit and then turn south on BIA highway 41 to the Nebraska border and off the Rez.

At this time, three things happened simultaneously:

- The blast and alarm had awakened the Rez police, and they were on their way to the vault site.

- Chris (FBI) in Denver was notified of the vault alarm, and the FBI helicopter was dispatched to pick up Chris at a parking lot near his high-rise condo in lower downtown Denver.

- The blast awakened Shappa (civil engineer for the Rez and volunteer firefighter), and the first thing she thought of was to get the Water Tender truck on the road in case of a fire.

Shappa told the Rez Police that she had the Water Tender and was leaving the town of Pine Ridge now. She was listening and communicating with the Rez police on the police radio channel, and they said that a convoy of vehicles was turning off highway 18 and onto BIA highway 41. She knew the roads well, and immediately she knew they were making a break for the southern border of the Rez at the Nebraska border. As a result, Shappa said she would try to cut them off. She said she would take BIA 32 and BIA 3202 west, which intersects with BIA highway 41.

Shappa had more road to cover than the convoy of crooks, so she pushed that old Water Tender truck to the limit. At this same time, the Rez police were taking heavy gunfire by automatic weapons (the Uzi's), so they backed off. They called the Nebraska Highway patrol and asked for a roadblock to be installed where BIA highway 41 meets the Nebraska border, where BIA Highway 41 changed its name to Slim Buttes Road in Nebraska. Still, the Nebraska Highway Patrol needed to organize faster. The caravan would easily slip past the Nebraska line in the next 20 minutes.

It was still dark when Shappa reached BIA highway 41, but she knew she had arrived at that spot before the caravan because she could see their lights up the road some distance away. She turned left toward Nebraska and then radioed to the Rez police and asked, "What are they driving? They should have beat me to this intersection?" The Rez police told her that the caravan had a large crane in the lead, followed by a side-dump semi-truck and behind them were two jeeps. The police said the crane was big and traveling slowly, holding them all back. That's when Shappa had an idea.

Shappa radioed back to the Rez police, telling them of her plan, and then she floored the Water Tender truck to a place just north of the Nebraska State line where clays similar to the Badlands of South Dakota were exposed on both sides of the road. She quickly turned the truck around, facing north, and parked. She hurriedly got out, attached the large hose, and proceeded to water down both sides of the highway with hundreds of gallons of water. It was a sloppy mess. Then she positioned the truck broadside to the road and ran to one side of the road while talking on her handheld radio to the Rez police, explaining that everything was set up.

The sun lit up the eastern sky a little at this time, and six activities were in full swing.

- The caravan was approaching the Water Tender truck parked in the middle of the road.

- The Rez police were following the caravan from a safe distance because the automatic weapons out-gunned them.

- Shappa was safely on top of a small ridge watching the caravan approaching.

- Chris was flying over Nebraska in the FBI helicopter. He was also in contact with the

Rez police and was aware of the plan that Shappa had arranged.

- Word got out to about ten bikers that were still camping on Ed's land, who were previously planning to leave soon because it was just too boring with nothing happening, so when word of a potential theft of the dark-rock got to them, they were off in a flash to back up the Rez police. They also contacted the police via handheld radios (nice ones, courtesy of the FBI).

- The Nebraska Highway Patrol nearly flew down the highway toward the Rez but would not arrive in time to set up a roadblock.

Shappa could still see the caravan's headlights as it pre-dawned. The first vehicle was a huge crane, and it slowed as it approached the abandoned Water Tender truck, but it didn't take long before the driver gunned the gas and drove off the south side of the road to get around the water truck. The crane traveled about 50 feet before the wheels, caked with mud, slipped and spun. The crane was stuck, and the Side-dump semi vehicle could see that he wouldn't make it on that side of the road. The driver panicked and drove on the north side of the road when his wheels started to slip as well, but he overcorrected and jack-knifed the rig. Both jeeps were following behind him, and one rolled as it tried to avoid a collision. The other jeep slammed into the back of the side-dump trailer. None of the eight men were injured, but Shappa could tell they were all panicking and running in every direction. One of them seemed to be the leader and settled them down. They all then grabbed weapons and took on defensive positions for the approaching Rez police, but to their surprise, no vehicles came down the road.

Shappa was keeping the Rez police informed of the events on the ground, and the Rez police eventually took up position on a ridge out of gunshot range but with a good view of the stuck vehicles. The Rez police explained to Chris what was happening, so the helicopter flew high and out of gunshot range, making large radius circles around the stuck caravan. At the same time, the bikers caught up with the Rez Police, and the police asked them to line up on the ridge overlooking the stuck caravan.

Nothing happened for 10 minutes. That gave the Nebraska Highway Patrol time to take up position on the highway just south of the stuck caravan. Everyone was out of gunshot range from the stuck caravan, but that didn't stop the militia from shooting in all directions, using their automatic weapons. They had pistols as backup, so they didn't seem to care about wasting ammo.

Time ticked by as all groups stayed in position, watching from afar. Shappa was the closest to the stuck vehicles, but they didn't know she was there, and fortunately, she could hear some of what they were saying. She could tell they were desperate, so she quietly let the Rez police know they could wait them out. After a few hours, the 8 men in the caravan were starting to show signs of weakness. They didn't have much water or food, so they could not last too long, and they started to feel trapped, and they were.

By noon, Chris had many FBI agents and vehicles in place on both sides of BIA Highway 41, and that's when the Rez police wrote down their phone number on a large cardboard box and placed it so the caravan people could see it. It took only 5 minutes, and the eight men surrendered to the Rez police. The police and the FBI cautiously approached the caravan and took everyone in custody. That's when the Rez police said they would take control of the area because it was Rez's land. Chris could tell something was up because he had gotten to know the police from the past, so he quietly agreed but stayed with the Rez police to follow their lead.

The Rez police told the 8 crooks that they were now going to the Rez jail and would be tried on the reservation for their crimes. This news scared the living daylights out of them all. They didn't realize that the Rez had their own justice system. That's when Bill spoke up, talking directly at Chris, whom he could see was the lead of the FBI. Bill asked to be arrested by the FBI and not the Rez. Bill said they would all confess now if the FBI got them off the Rez. That's when Chris understood what the Rez police were doing. After all, he didn't think the Rez had the facility to handle this many people.

The Rez police and Chris had a conversation out of earshot of Bill and his men, and they pretended to disagree and even shouted a couple of times. The truth was that they were just having some fun. In the end, the FBI took down all of the confessions and began to load up the prisoners. That's when Bill asked about his equipment. Chris looked at the Rez police and then back at Bill, saying, "When you get out of prison, you can take that matter up with the Pine Ridge Indian Reservation." Then Chris looked at Shappa and back at Bill and his crew and said, "It looks like you planned for a war with all of your automatic weapons, pistols, heavy equipment, and jeeps, but you didn't plan on a Lakota lady and her water truck. did you?" At that, everyone laughed, and many bikers were filming this on cell phones, streaming it directly to the Internet.

Newspapers and Internet news outlets caught on to this event immediately, thanks to the streaming video from bikers at the scene. Some of the headlines were.

- New York: "Don't Messz with the Rez."

- Washington DC: "Armed Militia foiled by Lakota Lady with old Water Truck."

- Denver: "Lakota Woman Outsmarts Militia Men."

- Minneapolis: "Pine Ridge Woman Sticks it to Militia."

- London: "Militia no match for American Indian Woman."

- Paris: "Armed American Men no match for Lakota Lady."

- Berlin: "Eight-Man Militia Stuck in The Mud by Lakota Woman in the US."

The news changed the perception of the Pine Ridge Indian Reservation.

The bikers still staying at Ed's place knew that no one would try this again, so they all decided to return to Sturgis and then home after that. They said their goodbyes to Ed and told him they would return next August. Some were a little concerned about Ed as he seemed a little slower since this whole episode erupted some time ago. The truth is that these last months were the best time Ed had ever had in years. However, some quiet time might help him get his strength back. Before the bikers took off, they cleaned up the place, chopped more firewood than Ed would need for the winter, and stored away the remaining food and water that was previously donated. Then they were off, and Ed went fishing. It was a beautiful October day, with a hint of crispness in the air, indicating the upcoming winter.

With the Rez and ranches safer now, the DRDC decided to take a temporary break from Friday meetings so that its members could catch up on long overdue work that was delayed due to the dark-rock activity. Equipment needed maintenance, small farmland needed attending to, and food for the ranch/farm animals needed to be prepared and stored away for the upcoming winter. Winter snow and cold temperatures kept neighbors more isolated with much less communication, but they were all looking forward to getting the DRDC started again in the Spring or early summer.

Ed told several DRDC members that since he now had extra money, he was thinking of driving down to Galveston, Texas, during the winter to fish.

Chapter 18: GOLD RUSH 2.0, BUT NOT FOR GOLD

The news of a new Super Element spread like the Black Hills gold rush from the late 1800s, with one main exception. Rather than word of mouth or newspapers, the information was spread via the Internet. This near-instantaneous communication to all corners of the world caused a mass migration of fortune hunters from all over the United States and the world.

All federal and state lands that offered mining rights were overwhelmed with requests, and even land purchases were happening at record paces. This activity increased the price of land by remarkable amounts, and the locals were shut out of buying land due to the price increases. The buyers were mainly US citizens, but an alarming number of people came from outside the US, and it was difficult to see what Country they came from because they were trying to hide their mother country.

The South Dakota Governor's office quickly realized the influx of miners and prospectors and immediately requested emergency assistance from the federal government for law enforcement and environmental protection. The Governor knew the Hills well and realized that this new rush to find the Super Element would affect all roadway types (asphalt, gravel, and dirt roads) and the groundwater and surface water due to sediment erosion. As a backup plan, the Governor asked for an emergency session of the state congress to increase fees and taxes relating to prospecting and mining in and around the Hills. There was no way the Governor was going to let this new mining rush destroy the Black Hills. The Governor's office even created a war room to stay on top of problems, issues, ideas, and costs associated with this rapidly increasing influx of people. Fortunately, Chris from the FBI was also alerting DC of the potential problems, and the President of the United States was made aware. As a result, Congress also became involved, and a special session was scheduled. This issue was not political, and even the most partisan members of Congress were on board to help.

It was not just citizens of the United States that were interested. The FBI had been monitoring chatter from outside sources and within the Country and learned of a huge interest in hiring people to work in the Black Hills for special interest clients. The FBI even learned of classified ads offering large amounts of money for miners to come to South Dakota.

Chapter 19: THINK TANK

Back in Washington, DC, Congress wanted answers about the Super Element asteroid material. They wanted to understand the value of justifying the FBI's activities and the cost to taxpayers in buying this material. For this reason, a Think Tank was created, which took place at Georgetown University and was administered by a well-known and successful professor that chaired many Think Tanks in the past. He had several great choices for the team, but unfortunately, that would not happen.

The massive interest in the new Element caught the eye of several politicians, and they demanded to be members of this Think Tank. This demand was to the objection by the Chairman, but it didn't matter because one Senator was in charge of the Defense Committee and argued that they must be represented on all defense issues. This argument opened up other politicians close to NASA and so on. The Think Tank was filled with politicians from both parties that wanted attention for upcoming elections, and they took the opportunity to advertise this as much as possible.

It was a week before the first meeting of the Think Tank, and most of the members of Congress were in their home states. This opportunity gave them a chance to talk face-to-face with voters. The new members of the Think Tank took this opportunity to brag about being on such an important team, even though they forced themselves onto the team. In any case, they would have town meetings, soliciting ideas from the public, but their real intention was exposure and being on the 6:00 news. This idea worked well, and thousands of people wanted to learn more about this new Element, and several good ideas came out of these meetings. One idea was to use it on computers. The Senator that took this answer promised to check on this application, but the idea was out of his head as soon as the town hall was over.

People were getting into this discovery, and the politicians could sense it; if there is one quality many politicians have, it's how to jump in front of a popular issue and make it about them. More town meetings are established, and the cycle of ideas continues, with the public having many good ideas and the politicians promising to look into them. Then the politician forgets the ideas before even leaving the town meeting.

After the town meetings, Congress went back into session, and the Think Tank also met.

The trouble occurred on the very first day that the Think Tank met. Several members objected to the simple rules, and the first full day was a waste, except that the team finally agreed to the rules, which happened to be the same rules the Chairman introduced at the start of the meeting.

The second day was worse. You see, the Senators and Congressmen & women are accustomed to having work done for them, and in this Think Tank, the work is actually done by the members, and to make matters worse, the Congress personnel didn't have any real suggestions beyond what Chaska (back at the South Dakota School of Mines) had earlier suggested. One idiot Senator suggested they contract the Think Tank, so they would only need to review it. Surprisingly this had some support, and that was when the Chairman was seen with his head down and shaking in total disgust.

The 3rd day was the beginning of the downfall. Several members of the Think Tank no longer wanted to be associated with this failing organization and made-up excuses for not being there, such as voting requirements and staff needs, and one Senator said his state was about to get hammered by a blizzard, so he needed to be there to help out.

The Think Tank lost so many members that it had to use its initial recommendations for the final report, which Chaska had recommended earlier. The Think Tank then dissolved.

The media was very interested in the happenings of the Think Tank and investigated it thoroughly. What they found was what occurred, a bunch of Bumble heads expecting someone else to do the work, from "expectations" by the Think Tank Members. After all, that's all they ever did anyway, by giving their "expectations" and making someone else do the work for which they would take credit, but that was not all the media found. All of the excuses that members gave for not being in the meetings were found to be false, such as the voting requirement from one member. It was found that no voting had taken place at the time. One Senator's staff was contacted about needing the Senator when he said they needed him. They said it was false and that the staff had everything in control. The worse was the excuse for an upcoming blizzard in one state. The media checked the weather for that day, and the entire state was sunny with highs above 40 degrees.

Of course, the media reported the truth about each one of these cases, but they were told it was fake news. One media outlet asked the Senator how it could be fake news about the weather in his state, and he quickly said he had an emergency to get to immediately. Later that day, he was seen having dinner and drinks with a female staff member; how strange!

In the end, it was Chaska's Master's Thesis that was submitted as the final outcome to the Think Tank. Otherwise, it would have been copyright infringement if they simply used his results as their final report. The ordeal was embarrassing and disgusting, but as usual, these members of Congress would believe that no one would remember it in a couple of weeks. However, this was not the case. The American public was getting fed up with political stunts, and all of these Congress Think Tank members were voted out the following November.

Chapter 20: ELEMENT SEARCH

When the FBI began their search in the Black Hills, the first odd thing was that they could not find enough air reconnaissance aircraft for rent. It appeared that all aircraft were already under contract. The federal government then brought its air reconnaissance aircraft to Ellsworth Air Force Base. Chris had learned of new technology that was capable of subsurface investigation for underground military outposts, and he thought this might work for detecting the Super Element asteroid material within the entire Black Hills. At least this might give a better picture of possible locations that they could investigate with ground-penetrating radar or geophysical vibration vehicles.

Individual prospectors didn't have sophisticated devices, so they often researched by looking for anything strange via aerial photography. This method turned up some locations of interest, and mining rights were often secured this way. Illegal mining on state, federal, and private lands also increased. Law enforcement had reports of gunshots forcing miners off private land, so this was getting serious and dangerous.

One of the bikers that Chris hired was also a weekend miner from Hill City. Ryan (aka Toe-blade) had been looking for gold for most of his adult life and hiked everywhere in the Hills. He had never gone to college and barely made it through high school, but he knew the land and signs of the underground structure very well. He knew a lot about different methods for

determining underground anomalies, such as
vegetation type, soil condition, rock types, etc.

…..

Ryan grew up in Rapid City and moved to Hill City
shortly after high school. He bought a home just off
Main Street and barely qualified for the home loan
based on his full-time handyman job at a local
restaurant and bar. Houses were cheaper in Hill City
than in Rapid, and he was proud to own his place at
such a young age. It needed a lot of work, but he
enjoyed working on his property, and when he
repaired anything, he did it right. He learned a lot
about carpentry, HVAC, roofing, electrical, copper
piping, insulation, roofing repair, doors & windows,
siding, and painting methods, as well as fixing his
appliances and, of course, toilet repairs. The
education he had learned in his own home made him
confident to help out some of his older neighbors.

Ryan quickly became friends with people in town
because of his job, and he liked hanging out in the
small downtown area. Ryan was good with his hands
and volunteered to help rebuild old railroad cars that
were part of the 1880 train tourist attraction. He also
helped some of the old-timers with minor home repair
projects. During one of the home repairs projects, he
noticed a young lady about his age who was the
granddaughter of the old timer he was helping. She
was with several other young ladies but stood out to
Ryan. They were from Rapid Valley and had gone to
Central High School (Ryan graduated from Stevens
High on the west side of Rapid). She was the focal

person of the group as they came into the house to get lunch. Her name was Ann, and the house that Ryan was working on belonged to her grandfather.

Ryan took his time fixing a window that didn't open very well. He found and fixed it quickly but pretended to continue to work until the ladies passed by him again. This time he looked straight at Ann and said, "You are terribly beautiful." Ann was caught off guard by this but regained her control and said, "Well, you're just terrible too." They both started laughing out loud, with the other ladies smiling and talking amongst themselves. Ryan then introduced himself, and Ann did the same. Then he just abruptly asked her out on a date. She reluctantly told him yes, but that she lived in Rapid Valley, which was okay with Ryan. They had their first date the following Friday night and got along perfectly. After the date, they talked on the phone, sometimes for hours. It didn't take long for them to develop strong feelings for one another, and neither one ever looked back after that; they were the perfect couple.

The physical distance between where they lived was a hassle. They dated almost every week on one day or another. After about half a year, Ann would spend full weekends with Ryan in Hill City, where she eventually got a job selling Black Hill Gold jewelry, some groceries, and high-end outdoor gear such as Lowe Pro and Lowe Alpine. This merchandise was a weird combination, but that's what was needed in order to keep the store open year-round in a small town. She started at minimum wage, but after the owner noticed all the guys coming to the store, he gave her a raise so that no one would steal her away for another job. Once she had her job in Hill City, she lived with Ryan.

Over the years, Ryan and Ann were considered naturally married, just not formally or legally, and they even talked of having children one day. That's when Ryan decided to get out of his current job and started working for the State Forestry Department just down the road from Hill City. This job was perfect for Ryan, giving him a better chance to learn more about the Hills.

This couple now had two good jobs and could afford more things. This experience was new for them both because they grew up relatively poor (middle-class poor). Ann bought a removable hard-top Jeep, and Ryan earned enough for his first Harley, and that machine became his second love. They never missed a Sturges Rally after that. Ryan and Ann were both in the Buffalo Chip the night that help was requested, and they traveled to Ed's place that next day.

. . . .

Given Ryan's self-education in geology, mineralogy, and structural geology, as well as his back road travel with his new job, it only took Ryan a few days to see one obvious hint of the dark-rock locations. It was a simple observation. He had purchased satellite images of the Rez and Ed's place and the entire area he knew around Hill City. The satellite images were taken in the summer to see vegetation, but winter images were also used to see the ground better after deciduous trees and shrubs lost their leaves. Sometimes the photos showed many snow-covered landscapes, which were the least usable... or were they?

Ryan studied the maps for hours, thinking of different ways to detect the underground material, and then it hit him. Sure enough, the locations with the dark-rock on the Rez and Ed's place were not covered in snow. The dark-rock must permeate or reflect a small amount of heat that affects the snow cover. This was the clue that Ryan wanted, and he ordered satellite images for the entire Black Hills in South Dakota for dates that he knew were snow-covered. Ryan and Ann spent every evening going through the maps and identifying all of the suspected locations of the new Super Element. Then, Ryan, back at his job, gave clues to his bosses about potential asteroid locations. At first, they ignored him, but after the first successful find, they started to listen to him. Ryan also suggested sites on federal land to Chris, and he was right 100% of the time, which was way better than what the federal government did with all of the aircraft and other sophisticated equipment. Ryan and Ann started to get a reputation with the nickname "asteroid whisperers."

On weekends Ann, with Ryan in the passenger seat of her jeep, secretly arranged to meet with various landowners to suggest a digging site for the Super Element. These meetings were always secret to protect the landowner, which was greatly appreciated. Ann and Ryan only sometimes learned of the results, but on several occasions, they were invited to dinner by some of these landowners. During dinner, they were given envelopes with large sums of money. You see, Ann and Ryan helped many landowners discover the Super Element on their land, making the landowners millionaires. The cash was a gift for making that happen. Ann and Ryan were becoming rich too.

Ann and Ryan were pulling in the extra money enough to purchase another piece of property, maybe for retirement or vacations. They loved the old west, and Hill City and Deadwood were always their favorite places, so they looked up old western towns with saloons and came across one of interest in California, on the central coast and only an hour from the beach. It was the old town of Pozo. They visited the tiny town and fell in love with the area. The old Pozo saloon was an amazing find, and on the Internet, they found an old picture of the Saloon with a small tree where the cowboys would tie off their horses. That tree is still in front of the Saloon, but much bigger now. Down by the neighboring Forest Service building was another old abandoned building from that same time period. This realization was hard to believe, so they purchased 25 acres in the area of the historic Pozo Saloon. It was perfect in the winter but hot in the summer, which was no problem for them. Summer is the best in the Black Hills, but can be a little cold in the winter, so it would be good for a change after retiring, and they could live a few months in Pozo and the other 9 months in the Black Hills. They would buy a fifth wheel or Winnebago for living in California. They'd live in the camper for a few months if they can't get a water well or septic. They had never been to California before, so it was a surprise that Rapid City was larger than any city in San Luis Obispo County. Even the nearby southern county of Santa Barbara County only had equal-sized cities of Santa Maria and Santa Barbara. To make things better, the northern county of Monterey has only one city the size of Rapid City, and it's in the northern part of that county. This was a big surprise because they thought the entire coastline of California was overpopulated. California certainly had a bad rap regarding the central coast near Pismo Beach, Arroyo Grande, and the rest of the five cities, plus San Luis Obispo to Templeton to Paso Robles and Morro Bay to Cambria. Now they had retirement plans with some of their money, but the Black Hills and Hill City was their primary home, and they liked their small downtown house so much that they didn't even think of buying something else. However, Ryan wanted a 4-car garage, heated, of course, so they had that built, and it was bigger than the house. They needed a space for the Harley, Ann's Jeep, Ryan's pickup, and an extra space for working on things.... perfect.

One evening Ann and Ryan were joking with each other about the richness of the Hills, particularly the gold within the Hills. Ann then had an idea for slogans at her work. She asked Ryan what he thought of her slogans for her job selling gold jewelry, "Earth To Earrings," "Rocks To Ring," "Mining to Memories," and "Soil for the Sole," and then Ryan started to get involved by saying "Bedrock to the Bed." That's when Ann threw a pillow at Ryan, and they laughed so hard it hurt. The conversation continued in a more sexual way, but none of those slogans would be introduced to Ann's boss the next day. Anne's boss really liked several of her first slogans; he had them copywritten and then used them for advertising. These slogans earned Ann a managerial job and a nice raise.

By the Spring of that year, Ann and Ryan were getting a little burned out with their jobs and research and finally decided to take a little time off. Ryan was an avid fisherman all of his life, and Ann liked it too. They fished on Deerfield Lake because it was near their hometown of Hill City, and they also liked that it was less fished than other lakes like Sheridan Lake or Pactola Reservoir. They liked them all and often boated on Pactola, but something about Deerfield always seemed the best, particularly in the early winter. Ryan and Ann noticed that Sheridan and Pactola froze over earlier than Deerfield, particularly after extra hot summers, and it seemed to them that the fish were bigger too. They thought some hot springs entered Deerfield somewhere, and that was about it. Deerfield eventually froze over, becoming a moot point until it melted first in the Spring. Every year was the same, and it was just normal.

One night, Ryan had a vivid dream about the dark-rock heating up the snow on the surface, and he had a nightmare of forest fires at Deerfield Lake. The dream was so intense he imagined the water in Deerfield Lake evaporating. Ryan woke up in a sweat and got up for a drink of water. That's when it hit him. He must have unconsciously known that a huge dark-rock asteroid might be buried below Deerfield Lake. It just made sense.

The following day, both Ryan and Ann checked out the aerial photos of Deerfield Lake when snow was on the ground, and sure enough, they could see an outline of melted snow on parts of the shoreline. They then ordered more satellite photos of Deerfield Lake from the past, going back ten years. They were all basically the same. This proof was amazing and good enough for them, but they would never say anything to anyone. Fortunately, few, if anyone, would put these clues together, so this was one of those secrets they had to keep from everyone. The lake itself was camouflaged for the huge lake-sized asteroid buried just under it. Maybe the lake was formed by the asteroid impact, but no one would ever know because nobody would ever study it. Ryan and Ann would then try to buy all land surrounding the lake, which would take years.

Ryan and all the other locals respected the Hills; after all, it was their home. Unfortunately, too many outsiders didn't see it the same way. They came to get rich, and taking down a tree or more was no big deal if they had a chance to find the dark-rock.

Most local people in and around Hill City loved Deerfield Lake, and this certainly included Ryan and Ann. There was no way that they would want this beautiful place to be torn up to excavate the asteroid material below it. The lake might be there because of the asteroid, but they would not let the asteroid excavation destroy the lake.

By reporting this information, Ryan and Ann knew they could be millionaires, but some things just aren't worth money. Living in the Hills brings on a feeling of freedom and a strength of faith in the natural world. Perhaps the Indian People were right about the Black Hills being sacred and the center of life on earth. Whatever your belief, most people get a feeling of solace if they stay long enough to hear the quiet and allow the natural beauty to infiltrate. Spending time by yourself in the Hills refreshes the soul. This solitude was always the secret of the Hills, but few knew it outside of the locals. Most locals in the Hills don't want attention given to the Hills, and many don't like the huge attention from Mount Rushmore and would rather it not exist at all. The worldwide attention from the Super Element is thought to be even more devastating. The last thing the locals needed now was the destruction of Deerfield Lake. Fortunately, only Ryan and Ann knew of the asteroid under the lake. No other person or group figured this out, including the federal government. The lake itself shielded the detection of the asteroid below. It was the perfect disguise.

. . . .

Rumors of dark-rock locations went wild then, and if someone even hinted at a good site, about ten 4x4 vehicles would be following that person the next day. Where he dug into the ground, those other ten would be digging near him. This excavation caused the back roads to deteriorate badly, and when traveled during rain or snow, the ruts in the road would become so deep that even 4-wheel drives would get high-centered and stuck.

The Forest Service closed fire roads, but outsiders would go around the gate or cut the chain and drive through. It was a mess for State and Federal lands, and to make it worse, several state and federal workers were assaulted when they tried to stop illegal activity. As a result, the state and federal workers were instructed not to confront anybody but to take pictures and license numbers, and law enforcement would take it from there. The state and the FBI started an enforcement list for future arrests once things settled down in the Hills. Until then, large encampments sprang up throughout the Hills, resembling homeless camps in large cities.

Pozo Saloon, California – Picture above by author

Chapter 21: SHOOTOUTS IN DEADWOOD AND HILL CITY

Greed is an amazing motivator, and the huge influx of people from all over the country caused pressure on rental space, food, and just about everything. Newcomers were camping nearly everywhere, and everyone had weapons, many with pistols such as the colt 45 revolver, Glocks, 9-millimeter semi-automatic pistols, and the list goes on.

Prospectors brought gold mining equipment but quickly learned that the Super Element would not be in small flakes like gold. The Super Element would be found in Asteroid-sized rocks, and this caused added pressure, knowing that the lucky ones could become instant millionaires while the vast majority would be flat out of luck. This realization made things worse, as the prospectors realized that you couldn't just pan the creek for the Super Element and that the successful dig sites would only be at the location where the Asteroid hit. Although the Asteroid may have broken up upon impact, the broken-off pieces would still be large and close to the impact site. This understanding caused some frustration and desperation among the prospectors because they didn't have ways to find these historical asteroid sites. Any word of a possible asteroid site generated mass interest in its location. It was cutthroat amongst most prospectors from out of State.

Too many prospectors didn't prepare very well and just headed up in the Hills looking for some kind of dark-rock. Then they would return to town in the evenings, thirsty for beer. The accumulation of outsiders with no ties or even respect for the Black Hills was alarming to police and all the communities in the Hills and for a good reason. On one occasion, alcohol got the better of a couple of tough guys from eastern states. It started with a minor argument and then shoving, and that's when they both went out on the main street of Hill City to have an old-time gun draw. It was 10:30 pm, and the crowd from the bars came out to watch. Other people were also outside from restaurants and just enjoying the evening. These two idiots actually did draw and shoot at each other from 50 feet, but unlike most TV or movies, their shots missed and traveled passed their intended targets. One guy was eventually hit, but so were two other innocent people just down the block in cars, and one was a 5-year-old child that died at the scene. The Hill City police got things under control with the help of good locals. Both shooters ended their prospecting dreams in jail for murder and attempted murder. After this incident, Hill City and other communities deputized some of the locals for help, and the Governor's office supported this with additional funding from the State. Federal money was also on its way as well.

It must be mentioned that not all prospectors were bad actors. Most were respectable people, just trying to survive and having a dream of prosperity.

Unfortunately, it wasn't just individuals from the United States that were in search of the dark-rock Super Element. Adversary countries were already in the Black Hills and were organized and nearly as knowledgeable about the Super Element as the United States federal government. They would search by satellite, research geology history, and travel on the ground to areas of interest.

Six months after the first public news of the Super Element, Russia had contracted three American construction companies that care more about money than patriotism. After all, in some corners of America, Russia is not considered an adversary.

Russia had much of the same remote sensing technology that the United States had and identified three locations of great potential. Each of the three construction companies was to gain mining rights, if possible, but that wasn't a requirement. Public land or private land, it made no difference. Russia was going for these locations regardless. However, it turned out that all three sites were on federal Forest Service land. The Russians had communications with the Mexican cartel and learned how the cartel grew marijuana on Forest Service land and used the same techniques. Those techniques were basically camouflaged during the day and working after 5:00 pm when most of the Forest Service personnel went home for the evening. The Russians were prepared to use deadly force if needed, so it turned out better if the Forest Service didn't know what was planned.

When first on-site, the Russians confirmed that only one site did indeed have the Super Element asteroid, and the size was perfect, not too big for transport, and yet big enough to make the project worthwhile. The Asteroid could fit on a flatbed tractor-trailer. They could electrify it to make it transparent and invisible during transport.

It took about a week to dig the material out and wrap it up so that a crane could lift it onto a large flatbed semi-trailer. The workers were sloppy in doing this, and they cracked the rock in many places, but the rock remained in one piece. All the digging occurred after 5 pm, with several scouts in case the Forest Service came out, but they didn't, and the roads to this dig site were closed by the Contractor so that no other 4-wheeler would see them as well. Once it was ready for transport, and after 5:00 pm, a flatbed tractor trailer and 6-wheel drive crane maneuvered the tight road up to the dig site. By 10:00 that night, the load was secure, and they slowly maneuvered on the road back to the highway. They were about 10 miles from Lead and Deadwood, so they parked the truck on a hidden dirt road with four security personnel, and the rest of the crew went to a hotel in Lead, South Dakota, to plan the path out the Hills. Once out of the Hills, they had an old barn to park the entire semi-rig. In the barn, they would break up the material into sizes that could fit into regular full-sized pickup trucks. Then the full-sized pickups would leave together and travel to Interstate 90 and eastward. Once on the Interstate, they knew they were home free for the trip up to Duluth, Minnesota, where a small cargo ship was docked and waiting for them. The cargo ship would then have several areas in Canada or the US where they could unload without suspicion. Then the material would be trucked to a port on the Atlantic coast and loaded on another cargo ship that would be bound for Russia. Getting out of the Hills was the last big hurdle.

The next morning the contractors left the hotel and met up with several Russian nationals. They had two vans marked "Jim Electrical Services" and "Romeo's Pizza." They could see at least 7 Russians that appeared to be heavily armed. The Contractor always knew that this operation was illegal, but seeing this made it all the more real, and several of the Contractor's personnel began to regret their involvement. In any case, it was happening now, and it was almost over.

The Russian vehicles and the contractors' vehicles met up with the flatbed semi-truck just as the semi turned off Highway 385, onto highway 85 toward Deadwood, and eventually onto highway 14A toward Sturgis and Interstate 90. One of the Russian vans was in the lead, and the other followed behind the truck. All seemed to be going well.

In the town of Deadwood, South Dakota, Highway 85 is named Sherman Street, and Highway 14A is called Pioneer Way. This intersection is right next to the main downtown street for old Deadwood, where historic taverns and the long-ago brothels resided (brothels closed in 1980 after being opened for more than 100 years - opened initially during the first Gold Rush in 1876). It was at this intersection that trouble started.

A few days earlier, Ryan and Ann checked into the Holiday Inn Express, next to the historic Saloon

Number 10 in Deadwood, South Dakota. Chris (FBI Lead) previously gave Ryan a couple of days off from his job in Hill City, and Ryan & Ann thought they'd enjoy a couple of days in Deadwood, gambling and having a few beers in the Saloon Number 10 (Ryan's favorite bar outside of Hill City and Sturgis). They had a room in the back with an excellent view of the intersection of Sherman and Pioneer. Ryan picked this room specifically because he knew anything passing through Deadwood would almost certainly go through here. Both he and Ann kept an eye out the window as they ate breakfast one morning. When they heard a semi-truck, they both looked down at it because it was loud with the motor stressing. It was a semi-truck pulling a flatbed trailer with other vehicles nearby. Looking closer, Ann noticed that the flatbed trailer was empty, yet the semi-truck was stressing like it had a very heavy load, and the tires indicated a heavy load as well. Ryan agreed that seemed too crazy and called Chris immediately.

Chris was in Rapid City then, but he sent out an alert (via text message) to all agents and contractors. He wrote, "This could be what we've been anticipating. All available agents need to go to Deadwood asap. Contractors in Deadwood need to shelter in place." Chris ordered a helicopter and planned on being there in half an hour. He hoped to get the truck and convoy trapped on the highway, away from populated areas. Highway 14A between Deadwood and Sturges would be perfect, but that wasn't going to happen.

While Chris waited outside his temporary office at the Rapid City Police Headquarters, he received another call from Ryan. Ryan explained that the semi-truck was having trouble negotiating the corner and that a local police officer was getting involved. Ryan said he had brought his Colt 45 with him and was going down to help if trouble occurred.

Ryan rarely carried a gun, but when he did, he would take just one very special gun. It was an early 2nd generation Colt 45 single-action revolver built in 1957. It was perfectly balanced for him and the most accurate pistol he had ever shot. This pistol and his Harley were two of the most valuable items he owned, and he often joked that he wanted to be buried with them both.

As he told Chris about the traffic issue, shots broke out, and Ryan grabbed his gun and raced out the door to the front entrance to Saloon Number 10, which was the quickest way for Ryan to get to the intersection and maintain some cover. Ann took the phone and said to Ryan, "you be careful; let the police handle this," Then she kept Chris informed of all that was happening while Chris watched his helicopter land in the parking lot in Rapid City. He stayed on the phone with Ann en route to Deadwood.

Rapid gunshots were heard throughout the intersection as Ryan ran down the stairway. By the time he got to Main Street in front of Saloon Number 10, the Russians and their contractors were in total panic. They pulled weapons and shot the police officer as he tried to radio for support. His message didn't get through as he was taken down with an automatic weapon. Two Russians had entered Saloon

Number 10 from the back door before Ryan was there and shot up the Saloon, hitting any patrons in their way. Then they waited at the back door facing the intersection of Sherman and Pioneer, away from the Saloon entrance from Main Street. This situation saved Ryan from being seen as he stepped into the Saloon from Main Street. Ryan, eyeing the shot-up Saloon and wounded patrons, lifted his pistol in the direction of the two Russians, both with their backs to Ryan and looking out the back door. Ryan walked as quietly as he could on the squeaky wood floor, and when he was 30 feet away, he pulled back the hammer on his gun. The distinct clicking caused one of the Russians to turn around, and while he started to point his automatic weapon, Ryan pulled the trigger and hit the Russian squarely in the head. Then, Ryan pulled the hammer back again while the other Russian tried to take cover and pulled his gun around while pulling the trigger, spraying the wall with bullets. Just before the spray of lead reached Ryan, he pulled the trigger again, hitting the Russian in the chest and knocking him backward and out the back door.

With the one dead police officer and no other officer in sight, the Russians tried to get the semi rig around the corner and onto Highway 14A. Ryan was at the back door of Saloon Number 10 and watched what was happening. He heard the hum of a generator on the semi-flatbed and knew something was strange. Ryan walked out of the back door and secured it open. Then he walked over to a small retaining wall and looked at the semi and flatbed. He was a long distance away for a pistol, but he braced his pistol against the top of the concrete wall and got two shots off at the generator before he needed to take cover. The first shot missed, but the second shot started shutting the generator down. When this happened, the Invisible Asteroid on the flatbed began to flash back and forth between visible and invisible until the generator shut down, making this large Asteroid fully visible.

It was a fantastic sight for all those witnessing this. The large stolen Asteroid was huge and an awesome sight to see. Now that the Asteroid was visible, the contractors' employees ran off and didn't want anything more to do with the situation. The shootout was not part of the deal, so the remaining 5 Russians were on their own. They abandoned the semi and ran toward Ryan because he had uncovered their scheme. Ryan was able to get one more shot off just before he reentered the Saloon. At that point, the Russians sprayed bullets all over the back entrance to the Saloon. That one shot by Ryan stopped one Russian with a strike on his right knee. He was in pain and immobile.

As the last 4 Russians stormed the back door, Ryan retreated through the Saloon. While he walked toward the front entrance, he saw that three other bikers had regrouped and had weapons ready. When Ryan walked by, one of them said, "We have your back, brother." Ryan then went across Main Street and stood there waiting for confrontation with the Russians as they walked out into the street through the main entrance.

The next thing heard was a gunfight in Saloon Number 10, as gun smoke spilled out onto Main Street. Only one Russian made it to Main Street and saw Ryan standing there with his Colt 45 in hand. Simultaneously they both lifted their weapons and fired. Both were hit. Ryan fell back onto a bench, and the Russian fell back through the Saloon doors. Then two shots were heard from within the Saloon as the bikers finished him off.

Seeing the gunfight from the Holiday Inn Express doorway, Ann ran out to Ryan, who was bleeding from his right arm. She leaned into him, stopping the bleeding, while the left side of her long blond hair became soaked in red blood. People from local stores ran to help Ryan and those inside the Saloon. Shortly after, the helicopter carrying Chris landed, and other FBI agents and enforcement officers arrived on Main Street.

The gunfight in Deadwood was over. Only one Russian survived, the one Ryan shot in the knee. Ryan survived, as did all of those shot in the Saloon.

Chris stayed in Deadwood but instructed the helicopter pilot to take Ryan, Ann, and two wounded bikers to the Monument Health Rapid City Hospital & Emergency Care. Other hospitals were close by, but the hospital in Rapid was fully staffed and equipped like any big city hospital, and Chris didn't know the extent of their injuries. He wasn't going to take any chances.

The massive influx of law enforcement was overwhelming, and the area was quickly secured except for the semi-flat bed with the Asteroid. Locals were hammering on the dark-rock, trying to break pieces off, and law enforcement let them at it. The local law enforcement kept the FBI away, and after Chris understood the situation, he called his agents back. These locals deserved a chance to profit too. Three hours later, the sheriff had the semi-trailer removed and secured in an undisclosed location. The dark-rock was a lot smaller than before. Fortunately, the cracks created from excavation made it possible for locals to get big chunks of the rock, and several were large enough to be worth millions of dollars.

The hospital staff at Monument Health in Rapid City was ready for the wounded arriving in the FBI helicopter. Three hospital gurneys were wheeled out to the helicopter with 15 hospital staff and at least 100 people watching from parking areas and windows from the tall hospital building. News of the Deadwood shootout spread like horizontal snow in a South Dakota blizzard, and the news media was there in force too. Traffic was jammed on all streets leading to the hospital. Everyone in Rapid wanted to learn more about this unusual shootout. While they were being wheeled toward the hospital, all three men lifted their arms high, and cheers were heard from everywhere around them.

The three wounded men were quickly brought into operating rooms, with hospital staff expertly treating the gunshot wounds and setting up for new blood transfers. Ryan's gunshot was not as serious as the other two bikers, thanks to Ann's quick actions to stop the bleeding. However, both of the other two wounded bikers didn't have immediate help, and both had multiple gunshot wounds with a lot of blood loss. It was touch and go, but fortunately, the hospital had the experienced staff, equipment, and extra blood supply to save all of the men.

Ryan was released within a day, but the other two men needed more recovery time. They both nearly lost their lives and spent time in the ICU before spending more than a week in recovery rooms. During each recovery day, these men had so many people wanting to visit them that the parking lot was filled with Harleys. When they finally left the hospital, it was a media blitz attended by hundreds. National news covered this as well, and these two bikers became instant celebrities with book deals and interview requests. The company Harley Davidson even gifted them new bikes during a televised interview show.

What happened to the surviving Russian and Russian contractors? The Russian was taken to a VA hospital in Sturgis and given care there. His injury actually saved his life. The contractor personnel that was helping the Russians didn't fair so well. In fact, they were never heard from again. Rumor has it that they hitchhiked on highway 14A toward Sturgis and were picked up by some biker ladies, but that's all. Their bodies were never found.

Back in Hill City, Ann eventually supported what she called her hair tattoo. It really wasn't a tattoo but was blood-red hair color on the bottom of the left side of her long blond hair. This coloring was her reminder of when she nearly lost her Ryan, and she wanted this reminder in order to enjoy every moment of life with him.

Saloon Number 10 in Deadwood, South Dakota
Pictures by author, 11.23.2022

Deadwood, S. Dak., Pictures by author, 11.23.2022

Hill City, South Dakota
Picture by author, 11.23.2022

Chapter 22: PROFIT IN THE HILLS

The past year wasn't a bad one for everyone. Many homeowners found asteroids the size of cars worth millions of dollars, and some locals in Deadwood were in the right place at the right time to chip off pieces of the Super Element asteroid on the semi-flat bed. Most of the pieces were at least worth thousands of dollars and much more.

During the year after the Deadwood shootout, new home construction occurred throughout the Black Hills, and most of this occurred on large acreage lots. Private land for sale within the Hills became challenging to find, and prices skyrocketed. Skilled workers were in demand, particularly those with solid recommendations and work history. The best and most experienced skilled people in all trades were nearly impossible to contract due to demand. Bidding wars occurred for those that had the best reputations. It became so difficult to find skilled personnel that some were contracted from Denver, Minneapolis, and Omaha, and they were given free motel rooms as a bonus to live for months near the job sites. This influx caused a lack of hotel space, which eventually created a building boom for motels and hotels in the Hills. This, in turn, pushed the demand for other employment areas such as engineering, construction in all areas, restaurants, retail stores, etc. The Black Hills was having a building boom like no other. Fortunately, this area had a four-season climate because this kept the incoming population under a little control. As a result, good skilled workers came from nearby states, such as Iowa, Nebraska, Kansas,

Wyoming, Minnesota, Colorado, Utah, North Dakota, and Montana. Actually, workers came from every region of the United States.

Many people didn't know much about South Dakota because of its low population and mainly rural ranching and farming, which turned out to be an advantage to state residents. Generally, South Dakota could be thought of as a family-oriented state with good and solid people. South Dakota didn't go through population Booms and Busts except for the gold rush days in the 1870s and, of course, the current times. Steady population growth meant that people were family oriented, hard-working and respected others, at least for the most part. The government at all levels was more transparent than in some larger populated states, and taxes were kept low. The main reason that young people left the state was for employment, but that was about to change.

Construction methods in South Dakota and the Black Hills have always been solid. Things are built to last here, and the 4-season climate assures this, but it was more than the climate. Good building practices have been a staple here, and some of the lost trades are strong here, such as real rock masonry and large wood construction. With the new demand for skilled workers, some of these older trades were brought back to life due to the demand for quality log and natural stone buildings. Three new construction companies were established. All are separate companies, with one in the northern Hills, one in the southern Hills, and one in Rapid City. Each was similar in that they learned the old-school way of wood construction and natural stone masonry. These companies all started Apprenticeship programs, and there was more than enough work for them all. These companies took off because these skills became important in many areas of the country for the sheer beauty of the construction as well as the natural strength of the materials. All three companies also partnered with a company in Paso Robles, California, for quality redwood and other wood not found in the Black Hills of South Dakota.

The growth in the largest city in the Hills (Rapid City) was dramatic. Two high-rise buildings were proposed to the city planning and zoning department. One was 17 floors and the other 22 floors. These would be the two tallest buildings in the state if constructed. Both buildings were planned as mixed-use, with retail on the bottom floors, and the remaining would be luxury condos, except the 22nd floor would be a restaurant and bar called BC's. BC's was themed caveman and cavewoman from the fossilized bones found nearby, but it was also Space themed due to the asteroids. A large telescope was planned for the roof and connected to a large TV screen. Pre-programmed stars and planets would be available from a stationary remote near the bar so that they could be seen in high definition at the push of a button. The demand for luxury condos was enormous for people from Chicago, New York, and other large eastern cities. Many of these people had made their careers in big cities but had ties to South Dakota. Housing costs were substantially lower than in other larger cities, and so many of the condos would be second homes for summer vacations, hunting, or skiing in the Hills.

Although the Rapid City Fire Department is Top-Notch, they were not ready for buildings of this height. As a result, city code was developed with robust sprinkler systems and egress requirements.

Another area in Rapid was bought up by a billionaire investor that was very interested in Rapid. This company bought most property in what was the old Star Motel or Star Village area. It's a mesa in the middle of town, and development on the mesa's edge would have spectacular views of lower downtown and the nearby Hills. Mid-Rise buildings were also proposed on the mesa to create views from all residential construction. This area only had access via two separate streets and became an exclusive and safe area in Rapid City. This developer directly conflicted with the two high-rise projects and advertised as "High-Rise Living Without the High-Rise." However, these developments didn't need to compete because the demand for luxury housing was so strong. Within a year, the lower downtown neighborhood and the Star-Village downtown neighborhood agreed to connect with each other with what they called the Rapid Sky Elevator. It was planned to be like the elevator in the Luxor Hotel in Las Vegas that traveled at an angle. But unlike the Las Vegas elevator, seats and holding bars would be installed to make the ride more comfortable. Both downtown neighborhoods would be given passes because it would be their money that paid for the elevator, but cheap tickets would also be available for other city residents. This corridor became very busy, and the Rapid City police department had cameras everywhere and quickly responded when needed.

Everyone did not welcome the growth. Most people liked the old Rapid City and the Black Hills before the Super Element was found. The mayor and Governor vowed to maintain the lifestyle of the past, but they all knew that this area was to change forever.

......

The federal government and all US citizens were also beneficiaries due to the applications of the Super Element that were going to become a reality. Some examples that were mentioned in Chaska's Master's Thesis are:

Strength and Thermal:
· Spacecraft
· Deepwater subsurface vehicle
· Cold climate structures on North and South Poles

Stealth:
· Stealthy aircraft
· Stealthy nuclear weapons

Strength and Electrified Transparency:
· Electrified strong and invisible shields (above and below water)

Companies worldwide tried to create this element, and some came close, but the energy and associated costs made it unrealistic, given the small amount created. Other countries could not compete with the United States in areas that used the new element. This disparity brought in a new age of cooperation around the world. As long as the United States maintained a real democracy and respected a peaceful world order, the planet would remain safer, at least when it came to significant world conflicts.

Chapter 23: MINERS FROM WYOMING, KENTUCKY, and WEST VIRGINIA

Once local landowners learned from Ryan and Ann that they had dark-rock on their property, they needed to find a way to protect it, break it up, and eventually sell it to the federal government. Some land owners would put out ads for mining work in the classified section of the Rapid City Journal and Denver Post, but this wasn't a safe way to find dependable workers that would be quiet about the work and also secret in what they were doing.

Unfortunately, one landowner learned this the hard way. He had hired a group of workers as if he was hiring construction laborers, and most didn't know the Hills, let alone know anyone else that was hired. He put them all up in a hotel in Keystone, South Dakota, because it was after the tourist season, and all other hotels were taken. The guys were hard workers but were less than quiet about the profits they were making. The land owner had arranged a percentage of dark-rock to be split with the workers at a 5 to 1 ratio, with 5 to the land owner and 1 to the workers. This arrangement might seem like little for the workers, but the price of the dark-rock was skyrocketing, so this was substantial, and the workers could get instant gratification by selling their rocks directly to the federal government at an exchange near Ellsworth Air Force Base. The workers were mostly honest but did sneak out small pieces found nearby from the initial impact of the asteroid, but the landowner was not worried about that because his profits were enormous. However, the land owner was worried about the workers spreading the news about his location of the dark-rock, and with good reason. Within weeks of the startup of his operation, he had several thieves sneak in at night to steal some of his recently mined rock. Fortunately, the rocks were very heavy, and the large rocks kept the thieves from taking any. However, they made a mess of the area, damaging trees and keeping him up every night. He contacted the Sheriff and eventually got the situation under control, but he lost a lot of trees, and one hillside was severely damaged by the thief's dragging one rock toward the highway. This landowner needed to pay for off-duty Sheriff personnel for 24-hour per-day security.

Other landowners took note of this, and so did Ryan. Ryan knew a few guys from high school that had taken jobs as miners in different parts of the country. The closest were coal miners in Gillette, Wyoming, and some in Kentucky and West Virginia. Ryan contacted them all and talked about forming a reliable group of experienced miners that local landowners could contact for help with the dark-rock on their property. The group would provide honest and turn-key work, from removing the dark-rock to selling it to the government. It would be an up & up organization that would provide certified weights from the original mining to the weight during the sale. The land owner would not need to do anything except pay a pre-negotiated percentage of the rock to Ryan's organization (aka "the organization"). The price would not be cheap, but it would provide safety, security, and secrecy.

The organization started slow, but land owners warmed to Ryan's organization with time, particularly when most of them learned that they had the dark-rock on their property from Ryan and Ann. In fact, once the organization was accepted, it needed many more miners.

Ryan's contact in Gillette, Wyoming, was the best source. It was learned that several of Ryan's old classmates from high school were working there because the money was so good compared to work in Rapid City. They were all good guys, and trust was easy because they had known one another for years. Plus, the money they would make was so good, nobody would leak any information.

Gillette, Wyoming, brought the most workers to Rapid. Still, other dependable men joined the organization, including a Kentucky family with three generations of coal miners and another large family of miners from West Virginia that had mining in their blood that went back to their old country of Ireland. All of these guys were solid workers, but with one issue. They were all coal miners, which is considered soft rock mining. The dark-rock is hard rock and requires different methods of mining. Fortunately, one of the miners with Ireland roots knew of a way to break up the hard rock using a process that he called Drill and Fill. Drill and Fill was just as it sounds, you drill a hole in the rock and then fill it with a special mixture. The mixture is made with cold water and a special powder, which are mixed until it has the viscosity of Elmer's glue. The unique powder comes from an old family formula that would not be revealed, but nobody really cared about the formula as long as it worked, and it did work.

The hardest part of the process was drilling the holes, and as a result, this occurred during all daylight hours. It was the critical path to the operation. After the holes were drilled and the special powder was mixed with cold water, it was then poured into the holes up to the top. Then they just waited for half a day or so, depending on the hole spacing and thickness of the rock, but eventually, the mixture would heat up and expand slowly until it would crack the rock open. Once the rock cracked, heavy equipment was used to complete the rock's breakup and load it into trucks that would transport it to Ellsworth Air Force Base with a military escort. The trucks would be weighed before and after delivery to get the weight of the material, and then the payment was made to pre-established bank accounts.

Ryan had five crews running all of the time. They were not his employees, so they could take time off if they wanted to, but every day meant good money, so days off were rare to nonexistent.

Ryan took a small cut off the top of the money that the crews made, and they never questioned his cut. Ryan arranged for their assignments, and he also rented the heavy equipment that they needed to break up and transport the material. They knew that they would be rich because of his reference, so they wanted to be on his good side to get referred to more homeowners, and rich they did become over the course of less than one year.

The work was dangerous, even for these coal miners, and the winter months made it worse. Ryan insisted that they all have good health insurance, and he fronted them the money until they started bringing in their own. For one guy, this turned out to be a godsend. Most of the rock would crack slowly or with just one loud crack. A few situations were more violent, and no one would know why. The mixture has specific proportions, and the crews followed them to the letter. It could only be the spacing at which they drilled the holes, which varied based on the shape of the rock. On this one particular time, the rock cracked as normal but exploded in one direction. Unfortunately, one worker was directly in the path of a sharp piece violently shooting out of the rock. It hit him in the shoulder, cut deep, and cut a major blood vein.

Shock and confusion followed, but one coworker pressured the cut as the wounded guy passed out. Someone called Ryan, and he was already on the road nearby and quickly arrived at the scene. They loaded the man in the back seat of Ryan's double-cab pickup, and Ryan sped off with two other guys who were trading off, putting pressure on the wound. Blood was all over the truck and on everyone in the truck. Ryan sped off toward the hospital in Custer, South Dakota while calling 911. The emergency room would be ready when they arrived with a full staff at the emergency entrance. The hospital staff took immediate action by adding blood and blood products. The blood pressure of the wounded worker was extremely low, but the hospital staff was able to keep him from passing out again, and he survived. He was in the ICU for several days, and the doctor said that he would have died if he was not brought to the hospital when he was. The doctor said that even one more minute would have been fatal for him.

Miraculously this guy was back on the work site within a week, but he couldn't be of much help in his condition. Fortunately, this was a close nit crew, and everyone stepped up to keep the project moving forward. This incident occurred on their last rock, and it was a no-brainer to give the wounded guy his full share of the profits for that last rock. After all, they would be rich anyway, and everyone felt generous. The injured worker fully recovered but had one big scar on his shoulder.

Chapter 24: BURIED IN THE BACKGROUND

Over the past year, many events occurred in the Black Hills and out to the Pine Ridge Indian Reservation. These events kept law enforcement and the FBI completely occupied. Little did anyone know that activity was also happening on the far western edge of the Black Hills in Wyoming. Most of the Hills are in South Dakota, but a small amount is also in Wyoming. In fact, Newcastle, Wyoming, is in a beautiful location on the west side of the Hills.

Just northwest of Newcastle, some unusual activity occurred early on, just after news of the dark-rock made it to the public. A couple weeks after the DRDC's first meeting with the FBI on Ed's property, two men traveled up to meet the owner of a large section of the property on the Wyoming side of the Black Hills. The property was mainly in the pines but also extended west, onto the rolling grass hills of Wyoming, toward the Rocky Mountains. The property is unscarred by human activity in a rural area. Most people visiting the Black Hills go to the tourist areas in South Dakota and stay in Rapid City or other areas near Mount Rushmore. The South Dakota attractions kept tourists away from the Wyoming side of the Hills, and this was just fine with many property owners on the Wyoming side. To have such natural beauty and still be just a few hours from a Home Depot or Ace Hardware, plus restaurants and good hospitals, was the best of all worlds. People that want total privacy with modern conveniences just a few hours away couldn't find it any better.

The property owners knew they were already millionaires based on his property value, but they inherited it and were never going to sell it. These land owners lived a modest to poor lifestyle because they were cash poor. They loved their life and knew they lived in a way that many Americans could only dream of, but that didn't keep them from wanting some of the things they saw on cable tv. A new 4x4 truck would be nice, and a trip would be enjoyable once in a while. So, it was an easy decision when the two men met with them and offered cash money to rent their home and land for half a year. The two men offered them enough cash money equal to what they could get if they sold the property outright. Half would be paid upfront and half in six months. The only catch was that they could not say anything to anyone and had to leave the property in 24 hours. Twenty-four hours later, the landowners were packed up and heading straight for the new truck dealership in Torrington, Wyoming. Then, with a new 4-wheel drive double cab truck, they drove down to Cheyenne, Wyoming, to rent a luxury room at the Little America motel. From this base motel, they would make many trips during the next half year. They were having the time of their lives, knowing they would still be able to return to their paradise in the Hills next spring. They felt good about renting out their property because the two men told them they were renting it for a private religious retreat and that the house and property would be returned unharmed. In fact, they said that they would not even go into the house at all.

Back at the property, activity started fast. Trucks were driven into the property both day and night, but they were spread out far enough to avoid concern by neighbors. Fortunately, neighbors were not of much concern because they were few and far between. Also, the place being worked had good cover due to pine trees and rolling hills. Work was concentrated in a low valley surrounded by pine-covered hills. It was a perfect place to excavate the dark-rock asteroid.

While the Black Hills was bustling with activity and shootouts, this valley in the Black Hills of Wyoming was in the background and unnoticed. The FBI didn't even think to go that far west because all of their finds were from around Hill City and out toward Pine Ridge. As it turns out, this location in Wyoming was the farthest west of any of the asteroid locations.

It took two months to fully uncover this particular large asteroid. It was massive and way too big for a standard semi rig, but that wasn't a surprise because the plan was always to break it up into small pieces so that they could truck it out unnoticed.

By December of that year, the asteroid was being broken down into sizes that could fit into the bed of an F-250 pickup truck. How they broke it up is still a mystery today. Still, by January, trucks were leaving the property traveling to I-80 and westward to an old military munition depot near Concord, California. This Concord location was proposed to be the new Oakland Raiders Stadium site, but the plans fell through, and the Oakland Raiders were sold to Las Vegas. This unsuccessful proposal made this old depot the perfect place to temporarily hide the asteroid. The hauling off of the rock continued through February, and the operation was being shut down by late February.

Remedial action was next. The large crater left by the asteroid was filled in by trucks loaded with fill dirt and then regraded with topsoil. The area was then reseeded, along with the access road they created to reach this location. Ultimately, it didn't look like it did before their arrival, but it was the best they could do.

By March, the operation was complete, and the six-month rental period was over. The property owners arrived home on time and met with the same two individuals that they had met with before. They toured the grounds and were told that a fire occurred in an area and was reseeded. They were given another $100,000 in cash for the damage and reminded of this agreement's secrecy. Then the landowners were then left alone, and it was over. The landowners kept their secrets but had to come up with reasons for the new truck and spending habits, so they just said they had an inheritance.

No one knows what country or organization headed up the operation, but a small amount of the material was reported to be in new computer design. It seems that the Super Element was far superior as a conductor than any other known substance and was much more durable with no temperature issues. Typical circuit design does not work when designing microelectronics because temperature and minor losses make significant differences. Hence, the design was much more manageable when the new material was found to not transfer heat.

A prototype test computer that had the Super Element material was found to be made in a new facility within the United States. This new facility makes and distributes computers and computer chips worldwide. The facility had several big high-tech companies as clients, but it was unclear if any of these tech companies were involved with this new computer prototype. When the Facility CEO was asked where they received the Super Element material, he explained that an armed courier delivers the raw product sporadically and that he doesn't even order it. The company CEO showed the FBI the supplies that they had in the safe, and the FBI seized the material. But the next day, it was returned with no questions asked.

An untraceable communication (UnCom for short) was sent by an unknown source, warning of repercussions if the FBI didn't return the dark-rock, so while negotiations continued with the unknown entity, the supply of material was not disturbed.

The UnCom to the FBI started by stating that all Super Element material for the computers was secured in the United States. It was also stated that nothing was sold outside the United States. These two statements put the FBI and the rest of the federal government at ease, at least to some degree.

The FBI communicated that it would be unlawful to sell anything that had the Super Element material outside of the United States, and that's when the UnCom stated that any plans for all sales outside of the United States would immediately stop. The UnCom then explained the advantages of the new chips for the military and NASA.

A week later, a small newspaper in Bend, Oregon, reported on an exclusive contract between the federal government and an unnamed computer manufacturer. All other communication then went silent, as far as the media knew. Later, an anonymous source leaked that the dark-rock material had exceptional computing ability in the harshest conditions with both temperature and shock resistance.

At the time of this book's publishing, the FBI is still investigating where the material is being stored, not so they can confiscate it, but rather to determine how they can assure its safety and security.

Chapter 25: CONCLUSION

The horrific events were in the past now, and the cities and communities in the Hills now had control of their area, and they also had full support from the Governor of South Dakota. The entire Black Hills of South Dakota never saw so much widespread forest and roadway devastation from the Northern Hills to the Southern Hills. Fortunately, the early fees and taxes on mining of the Super Element, plus the federal emergency money, would be enough to bring damaged areas back to near pre-mining appearance. Of course, it will take years and decades for re-forestation, but at least the Hills were now on the repair.

Many local landowners are now multimillionaires, but very few prospectors profited. The Super Element asteroids were located on private or public land, not in mining districts. The Super Elements found on State land were sold, and the money was used to rebuild all types of roadways in the Hills; plus, enough was left over for an enormous emergency fund.

Back in DC, physicists were busy finalizing the characteristics of the Super Element, and the results were very much like the master's thesis from Chaska. However, they still did not know why the material was not radioactive and warm to the touch. Military use was marked "Top Secret," so no information was available in this area. Still, natural speculation was of a new attack aircraft (combination fighter and bomber, similar in size to the A-20 from World War

II, but much sleeker and air resistant) that used the Super Element on the outer hull because electromagnetic waves were absorbed by the material, making the aircraft completely invisible to radar. NASA was more outspoken, though, partially to gain national interest in the space industry again. NASA showed a new prototype of a sleek space vehicle without any seams or windows. They played a video of localized electrification of 2'x2' areas in which they could turn on and off the transparency of the spaceship hull. It was impressive. It turns out that the electrification rearranges the electrons such that the hull can be made transparent or opaque at the turn of a switch, and the strength of the material doesn't change when that happens. The material doesn't transfer heat, and this reduces weight for insulation and associated structure.

A new solid fuel, invented separately by a European chemical company, would be used with this new spaceship to increase speeds far beyond that of previous space vehicles.

Although the hull was much stronger than anything in the past, the speeds this vehicle could achieve would be devastating if it came in contact with the smallest space rocks or even sand-sized material. For that reason, the new spaceship was flatter and had a much less frontal profile, but that made it kind of cool looking. It would rotate perpendicular to the direction of travel to emulate gravity at the end of the wing areas, where much of the human living and helm areas were located.

Meanwhile, the science community unanimously agreed to call this Super Element "Chaska126". With this honor, Chaska went on to win the Nobel Prize in Chemistry. After that, he took a job at the South Dakota School of Mines, making the Geology and Chemistry departments world-renowned, and he brought in a lot of research money.

What happened to Ed? It had been months since anyone had seen Ed; however, he said he might go down to Galveston, Texas, for winter fishing. Chaska and Shappa called his place several times to check on Ed because he seemed a little different when they last saw him. On one beautiful afternoon in early summer Chaska and Shappa made a surprise visit to Ed's place. Ed wasn't in his house, and it didn't look like he'd been there for some time, and he even had several weathered holiday packages on the front steps from neighbors. They also noticed he had many unanswered messages on his old telephone recorder, which wasn't unusual for Ed because he wasn't very good at technology. Everyone knew he didn't like talking on the phone. They then thought he could be fishing at his small lake, and from a distance, they could barely see his truck backed up to the lake as usual. Chaska and Shappa parked and walked down to Ed's truck, holding fishing poles, a six-pack of Grain Belt beer each, and big bags of Doritos, but they stopped short and dropped everything. As they walked closer, they could see that Ed had died months ago, probably before the cold of winter, and he was now a skeleton in ragged clothes. On the shore next to Ed was the biggest skeleton of a catfish they had ever seen. Shappa looked at Chaska with tears in her eyes and said with a crackly voice, "Does his face have a smile?" Chaska looked closely, and sure enough, Ed died a very happy man. His physical being became part of the wonderful and rugged land that he loved so much. He died in his paradise. He was now with Opa and his folks again. As Ed traveled to the next level after his physical life, he met many others from his past family. He also met Hotah and Wichapi, along with someone named Miha.

In a short legal Will that was found on Ed's refrigerator, he gave everything he had to both Chaska and Shappa and asked that the lake and stock dam always be available for kids to catch catfish and that his millions of dollars from the dark-rock be split between his neighbors. That was all he wrote. Chaska and Shappa did much more and created a 100-acre wildlife park for people on the Rez and those living off the Rez. This location is where the Friday meetings continued, but they became more of a fun community event. The remaining 80 acres were reserved for the future hospital, doctor offices, senior living, commercial, etc. They then split Ed's money with his neighbors, who many did not have any dark-rock on their property, so this gift made them rich as well.

Shappa also had her work cut out for her. The Pine Ridge Indian Reservation built a technical college with the best equipment available. They named it Dark Rock College, and all classes were transferable with both Chadron State College in Nebraska and the South Dakota School of Mines in Rapid City. The money the Rez had from the dark-rock was huge, and they funded everything with cash. The little community that Chaska and Shappa grew up in became a center for jobs on the Rez, which required new roads, a sewer treatment facility, and water treatment. They were all built as environmentally friendly as possible. The community stressed self-reliance, living close to the land without burden, and with education. This good advice was the future they originally learned from their folks, and they knew it was right. A museum was also built, with high-definition pictures of all the dark-rocks on the Rez and Ed's property. One of those dark-rocks had a distinct shape, with a hole in it, just big enough to fit an adult. Detailed explanations were included with other pictures showing the history of how everything unfolded, from the early natural look of the rock outcrops through the excavation and transport off of the Rez. The displays were arranged in an interesting and educational way so that local and national media completed several programs. This museum became a destination for visitors from all over the world. The museum was free to all, but it ended up being a money-maker due to voluntary contributions and tips.

The prosperity of the Pine Ridge Indian reservation attracted thousands of Indian people who wanted to become residents, but that was not allowed. The Rez knew who were previous residents and who were not. Only original Pine Ridge residents were included in the benefits from the dark-rock, and the Rez ensured all of these original residents benefited. Homes were fixed and repaired, and roads improved. However, a lot of the money went to building up the people. Long-term poverty is deep-seated in the people of the

Rez, and just as in all communities within the US, drug use and alcoholism were ruining lives. The Rez Leadership established a law that if anyone was arrested while drunk or drugged up, they had a mandatory sentence to go through rehabilitation. Rehabilitation occurred in a state-of-the-art facility with a lake view on 100 acres of land adjacent to Ed's property. This facility was nearly spa-like, and most of those addicted were successful in beating their addiction. If they didn't, the process would be repeated. Everyone on the Rez was worth saving, no matter what effort was needed, and they had the money to help everyone now. As in all communities, not everyone accepts help, and some would leave to continue partying. Fortunately, most returned seeking help, and they were welcomed back.

Next to the rehabilitation clinic was the site of the new hospital. It was planned to be on Ed's property to serve the entire community and not just the Rez. Entrances would be both from Rez land and through Ed's driveway location. Planning and building a hospital in any town is a huge undertaking, but it was more difficult out here near the Rez. There was already a hospital in the town of Pine Ridge, and they could have expanded on that location, but they wanted a hospital for the entire region, including people living off of the Rez. Ultimately, they decided on a new hospital that would complement the Pine Ridge hospital by adding additional equipment and bed space. They needed new doctors, nurses, and administrative staff and wanted many to be Indian people from the Rez. Pine Ridge Leadership Council offered full scholarships for anyone wanting a career in these fields. It would take years to realize college graduates in these fields, but it would also take years to plan and build the hospital. Shappa was glad the process was started, and she was confident in it becoming a reality.

The wedding between Shappa and Chaska was no surprise to anyone, but it was one of the year's highlights. The actual wedding was very traditional, taking place on the Rez. Only native people were invited, but Ed would have been there had he survived. It was said to be a beautiful occasion. But unfortunately, both Shappa and Chaska had near-celebrity status, so the media grabbed onto the news. Chaska made a deal with the media to stay away from the Rez. In return for the media giving them privacy, Chaska would allow the media to attend the wedding reception. This idea worked for the local news, but cable media was more obnoxious. A helicopter kept flying over the native celebration and nearly interrupted the proceedings. That's when a second helicopter approached, and it was going fast. It was Chris with the FBI. It is not known what occurred over the radio between these two helicopters, but the cable news helicopter took off as fast as it could, not even returning for the reception. The FBI helicopter also left as soon as the sky was clear of any aircraft.

The wedding reception was open to all and was on Ed's old property so the surrounding community could attend. It occurred at the lake, but Ed's old house was also used. So many people attended the reception, and it was a fantastic party. People from many ranches attended because they knew both

Shappa and Chaska well. They were also good friends to many on the Rez. Also in attendance were about 50 bikers, most were straight from Sturgis, and Ryan and Ann came in from Hill City. The bikers knew just what to do, as they had all camped there when Ed was alive. They were sad to learn of his death, but they all enjoyed hearing about the smile on his face and the huge catfish that he caught just before his passing. Shappa and Chaska then went on to explain more. They knew that Ed's biker friends would attend the wedding reception, so they told them that a Celebration of Life for Ed would happen the following day. They were waiting for them to be here, at Ed's place, to have a proper celebration of his life. The group of bikers liked this, and several let their friends know to come out and celebrate Ed. Then the wedding party proceeded. The party lasted most of the night, but Shappa and Chaska were not seen anywhere after 10:00 pm.

The next day, everyone seemed to sleep in, except a few that went into Ed's old kitchen and scrambled up a batch of eggs. Bread was toasted in the oven, ten at a time. Cold scrambled eggs and cold toast tasted good to people when they started waking up. Everyone was actively cleaning up or preparing to celebrate Ed's life by noon. Ed's burial site was next to one of the big cottonwood trees near the lake, and he was also buried with a very large catfish skeleton. This was the location for the Celebration of Life.

It was a beautiful day in western South Dakota. The days were starting to cool down a little from the earlier hot spell, and the nights were still perfect. The

Celebration of Ed's Life started slowly, but by 5:00 pm, the lake area was filled with people. Another group of bikers rode in about this time as well. Shappa and Chaska made an early visit to give respects before taking off for a week-long camping honeymoon. They were going to camp for a week at the Ice Cave in the southern Hills. It was a favorite place for them, knowing the history there. They stayed at the celebration until 6:00 pm, and that's when Chaska asked everyone to grab a Grain Belt beer in one hand and a Dorito chip in the other hand and to toast the life of Ed. The cheers could be heard for a mile or so. One biker was live-streaming this celebration to one of the smaller bars in Sturgis, and the owner was showing it on his big television. News traveled fast; within 20 minutes, the bar was packed, standing room only. Other places in Sturgis heard of the celebration and tried to capture it but couldn't get it going fast enough.

After Chaska's toast, he had a few words to say. He said," Ed was like a father to me. He was there when I needed someone to talk to, and we had many good talks here at this lake while fishing. I know Ed had a rough life, and many of you know how he lost his parents and wife, Opa, but Ed recuperated and was one of the most solid individuals I've ever known. Ed was always poor in finances but rich in those that loved him, and on the Rez, he's considered one with the Lakota people, the highest honor we can give him. Rest In Peace, my friend Ed". Chaska's toast was well received, and Shappa was in tears.

At this moment, Shappa noticed an old pickup truck driving into Ed's driveway, and she pointed this out to Chaska. Chaska and everyone else looked in that direction and moved out of the way as the old truck was driven to within 20 feet of Ed's burial location. The young driver got out quickly and ran to the passenger door to help an elderly couple out of the vehicle. They walked slowly up to the grave site. They stood there with Shappa, Chaska, and the driver for a long time, and you could barely hear the older couple talking in Lakota. It sounded sad, and you could see that the elderly couple was having difficulty accepting Ed's death. The entire crowd was silent as they watched this mysterious couple paying respect. Then, the elderly man and woman spread something on the gravesite and turned toward the truck. They held hands as they walked back to the truck. The driver helped them in the vehicle, and they were off again. As they were leaving, a big biker standing close to Shappa asked, who were those people? Shappa said that they were the parents of Opa, Ed's wife and that they were also Ed's adopted second parents. She said they were in their late 90s and had lost their only daughter and now their adopted son. It was very sad to watch. Shappa and Chaska took off for their Ice Cave honeymoon about an hour later.

After Shappa and Chaska left, other people said a few words as the evening continued, but other than Shappa, Chaska, and his adopted folks, all of Ed's closest friends had already passed. The party continued into the evening, and people learned more about Ed's life. It was a surprise to have learned of Ed's natural marriage to Opa and the sadness of her death. However, the bikers loved to hear that Ed had a motorcycle, even if it was only a Honda 50. In truth, most understood how hard it is to get a Harley Davidson. They knew Ed would have enjoyed the freedom of biker life, if he had the money and opportunity. There are a lot of different types of bikers that go to Sturgis. Some buy rides as a hobby and are professional people, like lawyers, engineers, etc. Others are gang members, such as the local Banditos or Hells Angels, but the majority are those who grew up in poor or middle-class families and didn't have much money while growing up. They might have started with smaller motorcycles, like Ed had, or larger bikes. Many started with trail bikes and loved to ride. Most within this group could not afford maintenance, so they learned to work on their own bikes and only brought them to the shop when repairs were more than they could handle with the tools that they had. It was this third type of biker that came to the aid of Ed and his neighbors.

The event at Ed's place was a good reminder of the DRDC, and it became an annual celebration after the Sturgis Rally each August.

....

Chris went back to the FBI office in Denver, but he would occasionally come back to Rapid City every couple of months to visit some friends. He became good friends with two Rapid City police officers, Maka and her brother Chaiton. The Word was that his late wife, Jen, had also known them, and when Ryan

and Ann learned of her death, they sent Chris a large
and heavy package.

....

Back in Hill City, Ryan, drinking beer with Ann and
other friends in a local bar, heard someone over the
crowd yell, "hey Toe-blade, are there any more Super
Element rocks left for us." Ryan looked over and saw
a good friend from Rapid City. He smiled, looked at
Ann, then looked in the direction of Deerfield Lake
and said loudly, "Nope, they got 'em all."

....

Interesting Side Note: It happened that the Super
Element was not the only valuable asset on the Rez.
Other young students on the Rez found prehistoric-
dinosaur fossils, and many fantastic dig sites were
eventually found. Excellent petrified dinosaurs were
uncovered for most known dinosaurs. This area
became one of the richest areas of dinosaur
discoveries worldwide. Within a few years, students
of Archaeology and Paleontology started to use the
same data from finding the dark-rock, including the
ground penetrating radar and underground
geophysical maps generated by the vibration vehicles.
It turned out that the farther underground they went,
they could see changes in ancestral river beds. Based
on fossils they found, they could even tell the age of
the changed river locations through time. They could
easily see the old river paths during human existence
and could also see the drainage ways from millions of
years ago. With this information, they traced rivers'

sinusoidal shape back to the dinosaurs' age and could see areas in which the river turned sharply, causing debris to be held back. Digging into these locations turned up many excellent dinosaur skeletons buried in ancestral flooding in which dead dinosaurs would get hung up cn tight turns of the river and then buried. Some of these new scientists started to think that the Yucatán Asteroid that killed the dinosaurs was part of the asteroid cluster that also contained the Super Element.

end

Some facts about this book: This book is fiction, but many places and happenings are based on real events. For instance:

- The snake with the skeleton head and real moving skin is a real story. The author experienced this firsthand with a good friend in the Bad Lands of South Dakota. When he thinks about this dead-moving snake, it gives him the creeps even to this day.

- Also, within the book, the locations described are real places. The Black Hills are truly a special place, and the author encourages readers to the reference below if interested in visiting this interesting area.

  "The Island in the Plains, A Black Hills Natural History," by Edward Raventon, 1994,

Johnson Printing Company, 1880 South 57th
Court, Boulder, Colorado, 80301

- Another experience by the author is fishing
  and hunting, and camping on land between the
  Black Hills and the Bad Lands. It doesn't get
  any better on a warm summer night than
  fishing and catching bullfrogs in the
  moonlight. This activity may not sound
  inviting or even interesting to some people,
  but the simple pleasures in life can become the
  ones that are thought of most in the busy life
  of the city. This is one such memory the
  author holds tight.

- A factual story within this book is the true-life
  Shootout with the FBI on the Pine Ridge
  Indian Reservation back in the 1970s. Google
  it for more information. A lot of turbulence
  and unrest occurred in 1975/76, the
  bicentennial of the United States.

- The description of the brothels in Deadwood
  is accurate. It was common knowledge until
  1980. Each brothel had a different color door.
  These brothels eventually became tourist
  attractions, along with the opium dens in
  Deadwood. It was obviously a rougher time
  back when Deadwood was established in the
  1800s.

- The first Saloon Number 10 was a real bar,
  but its original location depends on who you
  talk to. However, Deadwood is a fun place to

visit, and the current location of Saloon Number 10 is worth the visit. When the author was last there in 1979/80, it was a hopping place and crowded on weekend nights. It was a fun place, but it could be rough even back then too. There's a lot of history in Deadwood, and today gambling is now legal.

- Prehistoric fossils are very real in the Bad Lands of South Dakota. It would not be surprising that the Pine Ridge Indian Reservation would become a location for dinosaur fossils.

- The Sheriff will often have patrol cars on highway 79 between Rapid City and the turn-off to Hot Springs. Be careful with your speed on this road, but it's much better now that it's four lanes (two in each direction).

- Ice Cave "was" a real place. This author says "was" because the pillar of ice between the ceiling and the cave floor no longer exists, as it last did back in the 1970s. If you want to see what it was, just Google it. The author was lucky enough to see the ice in the summer of 1973, and it was a thick pillar of ice. The change is dramatic.

- Hill City is a real place and a great place to visit. You can see a lot there, from dinosaur fossils to trains from the 1880s.

- Rapid City is the second largest city in South Dakota, but it's recently also ranked the fastest-growing city in the Midwest. It seems more in the Mountain States than the Midwest, but it really is a transitional location, and that's why the author described it as such. The author knows Rapid to be a great place to live.

Author of the other books:

Not Intended for Humankind: Warning….Too much science for most people.

The research that went into making science fiction books did include years of reading books in both religions of the world as well as physics. Due to the loss of loved family and friends, research also included books into the afterlife.

This story takes place in 2022/2023. A man named Jim Zimberman and his wife of 40 years retired in Colorado just before the Covid 19 pandemic hit. Unfortunately, retirement becomes boring because of restricted travel, so Jim experiments with electromagnetic frequencies which he researched over the previous ten years. He wanted to experiment with electromagnetic beams, like the LASER, but not necessarily in the visible range. In doing this, Jim creates an elaborate computer program using known physics equations and stumbles across an unknown frequency (actually three frequencies) within the Terahertz Gap of the electromagnetic spectrum. What he finds is astounding. It turns out that the frequencies he finds create massive heat radiation. Just before he gets any further with his experiment, tragedy strikes in downtown Denver, Colorado, during an unanticipated clash between two extreme political groups. Politics in 2022 is much worse than during the 2020 election, and ultra-extreme groups developed on both sides of politics, leaving the vast majority of Americans in the middle with little representation. After a time, Jim gathers himself, but with a sense of strong revenge due to the tragedy. Jim realizes that he might have a way for revenge, and at the same time, he might be able to end the ultra-radical politics within the United States. Jim perfects his new weapon using the frequencies he found and builds it for long-range use to be as stealthy as possible. Then he plans for the kills, one on each side of radical politics.

Afterlife in the Higgs Field:

SYNOPSIS:

Have you ever wished that you could communicate with someone that has died?

What would you do if you could communicate through a cryogenic mechanism and video camera connected directly to the computer that allowed you to communicate with someone that has passed?

A retired engineer and avid reader of modern physics named Bret Zimberman created such a device, and he was in for the shock of his life and his afterlife.

The book "**Afterlife in the Higgs Field**" is about an amateur physicist who experimented with a super cold environment to see what happens when sub-atomic quantum particles stop moving. He wondered if the Higgs Mechanism (briefly explained in the book) would reverse and what would happen to the 3-dimensional physical world we all live in. As a result, he set up a camera outside the super cold area and then watched from his computer screen. To his surprise, movement occurred, and over time he learned that he was indeed looking within the Higgs Field (or an interim space between the 3-dimensional world and the Whole-One (Deity). He learned that he was allowed to witness the passing of the Sole of physical beings to what he termed the Whole-One.

Surviving Asteroid Storm Super Element 126: **Current Book**

Children's book titled **The Sort of Tumble Weed**: short book with graphics.

The Story of TUMBLE WEED (called Tumble for short)

Tumble was short and stocky and lived among the tall and thin grasses. He was lonely because he couldn't see others like him. What Tumble didn't know at that time was that he would soon soar with happiness and with many friends.

 Synopsis:
Have you ever seen anyone teased at school?

If so, you will like reading the book Tumble Weed. Tumble Weed was teased and alone, among others that he didn't resemble, but Tumble was about to see how wonderful things can be when he finds others who accept him.

Ultimately, Tumble doesn't tease back but wishes all others could be with him as he fits in with his new friends.

The book titled "The Story of Tumble Weed" shows that there are many different sizes and shapes of kids and that they all have good qualities. This book is a natural children's story, and I'm surprised it wasn't written 100 years ago, although it's more appropriate for today's young people.

Children's book titled **Old Red Number 1**: Possibly dated because dog racing is reducing in the US.

Old Red Number 1 was a racing dog back in 1912. He was horribly mistreated by his owner John Rotman, even though he won all of his races. Then, after a terrible accident that broke Red's leg, a group of young kids took him in and nursed him back to health. They also made a bet with John Rotman that Old Red would beat any racing dog he has.

Wood carving by Hilary P. Cole (WW II Pilot)

Sculpture by Vivian Cole (Artist)

He's really a rugged bass ain't he.

(How Ed was described by his Lakota friends)

www.ingramcontent.com/pod-product-compliance
Lightning Source LLC
Chambersburg PA
CBHW020243130626
46549CB00005B/2041